EVEN THE BUTLER
WAS POOR

Also by Ron Goulart

A GRAVEYARD OF MY OWN
THE WISEMANN ORIGNINALS

EVEN THE BUTLER WAS POOR

Ron Goulart

Walker and Company
New York

First published in the United States of America in 1990
by Walker Publishing Company, Inc.
Published simultaneously in Canada by Thomas Allen & Son
Canada, Limited, Markham, Ontario

Library of Congress Cataloging-in-Publication Data

Goulart, Ron
Even the butler was poor / Ron Goulart
ISBN 0-8027-5772-3
I. Title.
PS3557.085E94   1990
813'.54—dc20   90-38047
CIP

Printed in the United States of America
2 4 6 8 10 9 7 5 3 1

▽

1

T HE EASTPORT MALL WAS less than a month old and still had a fresh, not quite finished look. No one had as yet died in it.

At about ten minutes before the first death H.J. Mavity was glancing at her wristwatch yet again. Muttering, "Schmuck," she gave an impatient shake of her head and then started another circuit of the sputtering fountain on the ground level of the new mall.

She counted the mosaic tiles underfoot for a minute or two. Sniffed, with something less than pleasure, the mingled odors wafting out of the various open air restaurants—Señor Gringo's Mexi-Takeout, My Man Chumley Fish & Chips, Mother Malley's Oat Muffins.

Now he's eighteen minutes late, she said to herself after checking her watch again.

H.J., which stood for Helen Joanne—both names she was not particularly fond of—was a pretty, auburn-haired young woman of thirty one. Thirty two in June, a little less than two months from now. She was wearing faded jeans—faded by time, not the manufacturer—an emerald green pullover, and scuffed tennis shoes.

Twenty minutes late. Well, what can you expect from a man who intends to take you to dinner in a shopping mall!

This wasn't a date actually. She didn't date Rick Dell. Not any more.

Rick Dell. You should've known that anybody who'd stick a name like that on himself was only going to cause you grief and trouble. Plus an occasional migraine headache.

H.J. walked by Fritz the Furrier's, the Horizons Unlimited Travel Service, Niknax, Inc., the House of 1000 Candles. She hesitated in front of the Tanglewood Book Shop, then decided not to go in again. The fat boy who was on duty tonight had eyed her suspiciously when she'd browsed in there—exactly fourteen minutes ago.

What she liked to do was turn all the paperbacks that had covers she'd painted face out on the shelves. Quite naturally your average fat boy was going to be dubious about someone who came in to fiddle with novels having titles such as *Princess Glitz, Sweet Pirate Lover* and *A Passion in Manhattan.* But that was her specialty right now. Romance.

As far as book covers went. In real life, especially the past year or so, the romances had all been disappointing.

Godawful, in fact.

Topped off by Rick Dell.

How'd you ever allow a man who changed his name, legally and not under duress, to Rick Dell get close enough to touch you? she asked herself. A comedian at that.

The fat boy in the book store was eying her through the window, peering over a stack of half-price calendars. H.J. moved on, dodging three small teenaged girls with hair the color of cotton candy. She slowed as she passed the travel agency.

"Maybe I ought to go in and inquire about the rates to Devil's Island."

Three plump older ladies with hair the color of weak ginger ale almost walked into her.

H.J. returned to the fountain.

"What did you throw in there?" a plump blonde mother was asking a forlorn little boy in a chocolate-stained warmup suit.

"A coin."

"A coin, my ass. I see it floating there. The dollar Nana gave you."

The boy commenced crying. He did it in a very enthusiastic way, eyes scrunching shut, mouth opening wide, smudgy fists clutching against his narrow chest.

"Hush, shush," warned his mother as she leaned to try to retrieve the lost dollar from the blue-tinted water.

H.J. walked over to the escalators. That was when she saw Rick Dell.

Quite a few people noticed him at about the same time. He was stumbling his way down the upgoing stairway, coming a few steps at a time, slipping and being carried back. He was a tall, lean man of forty, darkhaired, wearing a grey suit. At that moment his face was stained with blood from cuts on his forehead and cheek. His necktie was undone and dangling, and several of the buttons on his blood- spattered white shirt were missing.

Dell kept fighting his way down against the current, bumping into shoppers who were heading in the opposite direction.

H.J. didn't move, didn't speak. She stood watching him struggle down to her. It bothered her that she didn't seem to feel anything. Not compassion or fear, not even embarrassment. It was as though she were watching this all on a television screen. The neighbor's screen, seen through a distant window.

Finally Dell reached her. He came staggering off the wrong way escalator, his skin almost dead white and his blood a glittering crimson in the harsh mall lighting.

He caught at her arm. "Sorry . . . I'm . . ."

The first thing she said to him was, "Where's my money? You promised to pay back the $5,000 tonight, Rick."

His eyes were glazed, not quite seeing her. "Money . . . thought I'd get it . . . and a lot more . . . but they screwed me up . . ."

People were starting to gather, muttering and murmuring. Dell became aware of the crowd growing around them. He put a hand on her arm, a hand that was splotched with small raw burns. "Listen, H.J., you can . . . if you're careful . . . got to be careful . . . not like me . . . you can make a lot of money . . . what I owe you . . . and more . . ."

She finally thought to ask, "Rick, what's happened to you?"

"You have to get hold of what . . . I have . . . and use it . . . understand?"

"Are you telling me you have my money stashed away somewhere?"

"Too many people . . . too many ears . . . All you have to do to find it is . . . remember this." His grip on her arm tightened. "Ninety nine clop clop."

"What?"

"Ninety nine clop clop."

His hand started sliding down her arm and, just shy of her wrist, let go.

"What the hell, Rick, does that mean?"

Dell sagged, then knelt. He swayed a few times, coughed twice, toppled over onto the mosaic tiles and was still. H.J. knew at once that he was dead.

Someone else was saying something to her.

"What?"

"Do you know him?" asked a frail old man, pointing down.

Momentarily distracted by the old man's glaring Hawaiian shirt, H.J. glanced from him to the sprawled body of Rick Dell. "Why, no," she answered, shaking her head a bit too vigorously. "I don't, no. He simply came up to me and started talking, poor man."

"I think he's hurt bad," observed a pudgy teenage boy, starting to squat beside the dead man.

H.J. suggested, "We'd better get the security guards to help him."

"Good idea," agreed the old man, wiping his spectacles on his shirt tail. "I saw one over yonder by the hot dog stand."

"I'll go fetch him," volunteered H.J., pivoting and pushing her way through the bystanders.

She reached the stand in less than three minutes and kept going. She headed from there to the ground level parking lot and her secondhand Porsche.

She didn't run, but she walked very fast.

Possessing not a shred of extrasensory perception, Ben Spanner wasn't at all anticipating what was about to befall him.

He was in the large white kitchen of his recently acquired house in Brimstone, Connecticut. A sandyhaired, almost plump man of thirty- seven, just a fraction short of five-foot eight, Ben, who wore a navy blue apron over his denim slacks and candystriped shirt, was seated on a stool and consulting a paperback cookbook. "Okay, Ceylon Chicken Curry, here we go," he said aloud. "One teaspoonful of ground turmeric." He left the stool and crossed over to the as yet unused spice cabinet and the wall near the sink. "Oregano, dill, anise . . . Where, sahib, is my cursed turmeric?"

He delivered this last in a singsong Indian voice, one he'd adapted from an old Peter Sellers characterization.

He'd have to watch that tonight. Some women didn't like voices.

"Even my wife didn't."

Although that wasn't the reason for the divorce. Well, not the main one.

"Ah, here it is. Turmeric." He clutched up the small bottle.

What was next?

"One dessertspoonful of ground coriander or a handful of picked green coriander leaves.

"Too late to trek out into the coriander fields to pick some tonight, old chap," he added in a clipped British raj accent. "Better locate the bottled stuff. Righto, here she is."

The door chimes sounded suddenly and unexpectedly.

According to the bright brass clock over the handsome new stove the time was just 8:15. A good fifteen minutes before his dinner date was due to show up. She was usually late besides, and you always heard her driving her Mercedes in.

"Even so." Shedding the apron he went sprinting out of the kitchen and up the side staircase to the bathroom in the master bedroom. He grabbed the new aftershave, *Jungleman*, and slapped some on his cheeks. For good measure he tried a little in each armpit.

Back down the stairs, two steps at a time.

After brushing at his hair with his palm, Ben tried a few smiles out, settling for one that mingled surprise, sedate lust, and a bit of country squire. He yanked the wide white front door open.

"No, nope, not having any," he said when he saw who was standing out there on his welcome mat. "Shoo, go away, scram, begone." He slammed the door shut.

Pounding started. "C'mon, Ben. This is important."

Scowling, he opened the door an inch. "Mister Ben, him just leave for expedition to find the headwaters of the Orinoco, missy. Everybody in servant quarters gottum black plague, except me. I got blue plague with polka dots and moon—"

"This is serious," H.J. Mavity told him. "I have to talk to you."

"You had your chance."

"Look, just because we've been divorced for two years doesn't mean we—"

"Three years."

"Two and a half exactly. The point now is—"

"Three. See, this is just exactly how it was during our ten turbulent years of marriage, H.J. You were always arguing."

"I don't consider it arguing to state the simple fact that we've been divorced for exactly two and a half years," she said. "I didn't track you here, though, to debate the—"

"All you ever did during the bleak decade we were together was argue and sleep around."

She held up a forefinger.

"That's the wrong finger," he said.

"I mean *one*."

"What? You only slept with one guy at a time? Well, I suppose that's a bless—"

"I mean I was unfaithful to you exactly once, Ben. Whether you care to . . . what's that awful odor? Did your cat die?"

"My new aftershave. A very sultry sort of—"

"I admit, sure, I did sleep with Guapo Garcia while you and I were married, but that was only because you—"

"Guapo Garcia. Right, it's all coming back to me now. You always made me a cuckold with guys with silly names."

"Guapo Garcia isn't a silly name for an actor, especially for an actor who happened to be starring in television show called 'Manhattan Eye' at the time."

"No more time for nostalgia, you have to depart. I'm expecting a— "

"There I was, with one pitiful little affair. You on the other hand, Ben, were out crosspollenating most of New England. You're the only man I know who went through his midlife crisis at the age of twenty-eight. I think you started philandering while I was paying off the minister who—"

"I never philandered, not once. You simply got the demented notion that every time I had lunch with an agent or some lady from an ad agency who was interested in hiring me for voice work I was actually in the sheets. Whereas I was really just furthering my career, struggling to earn enough to—"

"Can you afford to live in this new place, by the way?"

"I've been earning $200,000 a year since we parted three years ago. I'm just about the hottest voice man in—"

"Buying or renting?"

"Buying."

H.J. shrugged. "It's pink."

"I intend to repaint. Okay, it's been nice to see you again after all these years. Now scoot off my doorstep."

"I have a problem."

"Take it up with one of your many suitors. I am no longer—-"

"If I didn't have to come here to see you, I wouldn't have," his ex-wife informed him. "The thing is, Ben, there's a show business angle to this murder, a comedy angle I think. Since

you know a lot about comedy routines and old jokes I—"
"Murder?"
She nodded. "Could I maybe come inside? Is the house pink inside, too?"
He backed away, opening the door wider. "Mostly white," he answered. "What murder?"
She walked into a big living room off the hall. After glancing briefly around, she settled in a low black armchair. "This room almost shows taste."
"That is another less than admirable habit of yours," he told her, stalking into the room. "You start a conversation and then drift off into—"
"Okay, I'm sorry. It isn't every night my date falls dead in the Eastport Mall."
"How was he killed?"
"I don't know. But judging from all the blood and everything— well, he maybe was knifed or just beaten to death. Tortured, too."
Ben lowered himself slowly onto his white sofa. "What did the police say?"
"How should I know? I get the heck out of there as soon as he hit the tiles."
He watched her for a few seconds. "You left the love of your life lying dead in the middle of a shopping plaza and just walked away?"
"He's not exactly somebody I'm all that fond of," H.J. explained. "What I mean is—well, I did date him quite a bit a few months ago and then only infrequently. Back before I realized what a schmuck he was, I loaned him some money."
"How much?"
"A goodly sum."
"In round numbers, H.J.?"
She coughed into her hand. "Well, $5,000."
"Where'd you get that kind of—"
"I've been doing damn well since we divorced, too." She folded her arms under her breasts. "I usually don't go around loaning it out, though, but he said these loansharks were going to break his legs or worse if—"

"Obviously they did more than break his legs," he said. "As I understand commerce in this country, most loan-sharks are connected with the Mafia. So maybe the best thing for you to do is forget all about this . . . what's his name anyway?"

"Rick Dell. And he implied—"

"That's even better than Guapo Garcia."

"It isn't his real name."

"It isn't anybody's real name."

H.J. said, "Ben, will you sit absolutely still and just simply listen to me for awhile, please?"

"Sure, okay. Except I'm expecting my date to arrive at any—"

"Just sit and listen. Rick phoned me this afternoon, told me he was certain to have my money for me by tonight. He sounded very elated and pleased with himself."

"And he arranged to meet you at that new mall to pay you?"

"He said we could have a quick dinner there and then he'd hand over the money, yes."

"Was he dead when you got there?"

"Nope, but he was dying. He came down an up escalator. He looked really terrible and then he fell down. I knew right off he was dead, from the way he looked lying there."

"Did he, do you know, have your money with him?"

"He told me he didn't."

"Then maybe the guy got jumped in the parking lot, mugged and—"

"Not that parking lot, Ben. They have all kinds of security people prowling it."

He leaned back in his chair. "What else did Rick Dell tell you before he died?"

She said, "Now we're getting to the reason I came to you. I guess we've always had different opinions about your career. But you are, more or less, in show business and you do know quite a lot about comedy and jokes and the—"

"Wait now." He held up a hand. "Did this guy give you some kind of dying message?"

"That's what you could call it I suppose," she admitted, nodding. "See, I'm pretty certain he wanted me to have my money. He was trying to tell me where he'd hidden it." She crossed her legs, brushed at a speck on the knee of her jeans. "But he was uneasy about all the people, shoppers and all, who were gathering around. He tried to tell me, but he passed the information on in a way that only I would understand."

"So?"

She spread her hands wide. "I didn't understand him."

"But you think I would?"

"Rick was a comedian, not a very good one. He played small clubs— what are known technically as toilets—in Connecticut, New Jersey and, sometimes, in Manhattan. He was forever telling me old jokes, awful stories he claimed were classics. I never paid much attention to them, tuning him out whenever—"

"Yep, I'm aware of the gift you have for not listening."

"I'm afraid poor Rick thought I'd paid more attention to him than I did," she said. "The clue he passed on to me is, I'm near certain, part of one of those old jokes he used to tell me."

"He couldn't have just said, 'I hid the dough in my old boots.' Life, the world, everything would be much simpler if people didn't try to get cute—"

"He was dying afterall, Ben, which probably affects your judgement. You have to allow people to be a little dippy when they're—"

"Okay, what exactly did he say to you?"

She rested her hands on her knees. "Ninety nine clop clop."

"Beg pardon?"

"Well, his dying words were ninety nine clop clop," she said, a bit forlornly. "I know that's right, because I asked him to repeat it."

"Of course you did." He stood up. "Remind me to die alone in some remote spot."

"Well?" She made a vague urging motion with her right hand. "Ninety nine clop clop."

"It rings a vague bell, H.J." He shook his head, frowning. "But I'm not getting anything definite. Maybe if I—"

"Isn't it part of a joke, a punchline or—"

"Probably it is an old joke," he agreed. "In fact, I'm pretty certain it is. Suppose I think this over and phone you after my dinner date is over and maybe—"

"It'll be dawn by then. I don't want to wait all night while you frolic with some—"

"Hey, when clients consult Sherlock Holmes or Charlie Chan, they have to put up with the detective's little eccentricities."

"Charlie Chan never kept a client cooling her heels while he hopped in the sack with some bimbo."

"Which is why he ended up a bitter, aphoristic old man. Now then, you scoot on home so I—"

From outside came a combination of unnerving sounds. A rattling skid, a screech of brakes, a thumping smash.

"That must be Candy." Ben ran for the front door.

"Candy? That's her name? Candy?"

"Everybody can't have initials. Did you leave your car in the driveway?"

"As opposed to what—parking it atop your gazebo? Of course I . . . Oh, shit." She ran to the door after him, and looked out into the night.

"Candy tends to hit things that are left in the driveway."

"So I see."

$\triangledown$

2

SHE WAS SITTING, FORLORNLY, in the least comfortable chair in the small parlor of her small cottage, staring vaguely in the direction of the television screen.

A voice inside the set announced, "We'll be back to tonight's Multimillion Dollar Movie, *Philo Vance's Secret,* after these messages."

A portly, jovial man of about fifty appeared on the screen. He was attired as a very correct butler and holding a fish up in one white-gloved hand. "Chumley here. For another bit of chitchat about My Man Chumley Fish & Chips, don't you know."

The door chimes, a bit out of tune, sounded.

H.J. stood up and used the remote control box that she realized she was holding in her left hand to kill the set. Stepping around an upended chair and over a scatter of paperbacks, she went out into the small narrow hallway.

Not opening the door, she called out, "Identify yourself."

"Hell, I've forgotten the password. It's been three years."

"Oh, Ben." She unhooked the chain, unlocked the door, tugged it open. "I was hoping it was you. C'mon in, please."

"Maybe I ought to wait until your cleaning lady shows up." He came into the hall, stooped and righted a toppled floor lamp.

"It's worse in the parlor," she said, motioning him to follow. "Well, actually it's worst of all in my damn studio. They squirted about six tubes of paint all over the floor. When I saw that, I decided to postpone cleaning up for a spell."

Ben paused on the threshold of the parlor, taking in the overturned furniture, the emptied bookshelves, the pulled out drawers, and scattered papers. "I wasn't expecting this much chaos from what you said over the phone I—"

"What I was attempting to do was sound calm. But it's obvious somebody thoroughly searched my place while I was out at the mall and then visiting you."

"Looking for what? The money your boyfriend was trying to tell you about?"

"Must be something like that, yes. That seems logical to me anyway."

He eyed her. "H.J., thus far we have a possible murder—By the way, on the drive over I tried all the local stations and didn't catch any news about Rick Dell's death. Fact, mostly I got enthusiastic rock music," he said. "Okay, back to the point. Murder, loan sharks, organized crime. On top of that we now have your cottage being tossed. Instead of an ex-husband, what you need is the police."

"You don't have to get further involved in this. I only phoned you because I was upset and we'd been talking about the—"

"Hey, I'm not trying to abandon you while you're in distress," Ben assured her. "Besides, I've got nothing better to do. Candy decided to go home right after you called."

"I'm sorry. I don't really think, though, that my phoning you had much to do with it. She seemed pretty unsettled after crashing headlong into my innocent parked car."

"That contributed to her depression, yes," he said. "It also turns out she's allergic to chicken."

"With a beak like hers you'd think she . . . ah, but I shouldn't let myself get sidetracked. Really, Ben, I would like to discuss my problem with you."

Crouching, he started gathering up the paperbacks that had been dumped on the parlor floor. "Ah, here's my

Nietsche." He slipped that one into his hip pocket. "Your problem, H.J., can't be solved by civilians. I was part of a show for the Friends of the Brimstone Police a year or so ago. I know a few—"

"No." She shook her head, bending to put a chair upright. "I want my 5,000 first. The police, if they start nosing around, are surely going to confiscate any cash they come across. Tag it 'Exhibit A' and lock it away." She retrieved a fallen Tiffany lamp, replaced it on a reading table. "Besides, Ben, so far nobody in the law and order profession connects me with Rick Dell. If I contact your cop cronies—"

"They're not cronies. Just a couple of detectives I met, but they seem—"

"After we figure out the dying message and find my money, then I'll talk to your buddies in blue."

"Tan."

"Hum?"

"Brimstone police uniforms are tan." He carried an armload of books over to a shelf. "I see you still haven't mastered alphabetical order." He deposited the books, arranged them haphazardly. "Do you have someplace else you can stay, at least tonight?"

"I'm staying right here," she told him. "They've gone through the whole damn cottage, so there doesn't seem to be any reason to come back again."

"They might want to grab you."

"They could've done that when I came home an hour ago." She ran one hand through her long auburn hair. "Nope, the breaking and entering phase is over."

After replacing another load of books, Ben said, "Something small."

"What they're hunting for, you mean?"

"Right, it has to be small enough to fit in a book, a drawer—or even inside a tube of paint."

H.J. said, "I think squirting the paint was just for spite. I've got nearly a hundred other tubes and they only squished a half dozen. But it probably is something not too large they're after."

He sat on the arm of a rocker. "This doesn't sound like thousands of dollars in cash."

"Could be a check, though, or bonds."

Getting up, he walked over to her. "Are you sure the guy wasn't into some kind of drug dealing?"

"Yes, Ben. This isn't 'Brimstone Vice'."

"Even so, going to the cops will—"

"Listen, let's concentrate on the dying message first. Have you solved that yet?"

"No, but I was going over it while I was driving over here and . . . and . . ."

"And what?"

Frowning, he answered, "Nothing actually. Well, more than nothing, but not exactly something yet. For an instant just now I had an impression I was about to remember where I heard that phrase before. Ninety nine clop clop."

She watched him anxiously, reached out to squeeze his arm encouragingly. "Don't give up, you're getting warm."

He contemplated for a silent moment or two. "Nope. Nothing." He shook his head. "Have you had dinner?"

"Not exactly."

"Are you up to it?"

"I suppose. But I'm not in the mood for chicken."

"I never got around to fixing that anyway."

"I hear Orlando's is still in business."

"That place in Westport we used to go to years ago, near the Sound?"

"That Orlando's, yes."

"They weren't too expensive as I recall."

"You're affluent now, so it won't matter if they are expensive."

"True."

"Want to try it?"

"We'll at least get this room cleaned up first, then drive over. Okay?"

H.J. smiled at him, a bit tentatively. "Okay."

▽

3

THE VIEW HAD BEEN modified. Now instead of just a stretch of gritty beach and the night waters of the Sound, you saw part of the neon outline of the new Tudor-style My Man Chumley Fish & Chips restaurant that had been built just down the road from Orlando's.

"Well, we've changed some, too," observed H.J., lifting her glass of red wine to click against his glass of white.

"Same tablecloths," Ben said. "I recognize this patch among the checks."

The main dining room was large and less than a third filled. Their waiter, a frail old man in an oversized tuxedo, was standing over by a waterside window staring out into the night.

"Butlers," said Ben, glancing in the direction of the fish & chips place. "My favorite old joke about butlers is the one where the little girl in Beverly Hills is asked to write a composition about poverty. When the teacher calls on her, she reads it aloud. 'This is about a very poor family. The father was poor, the mother was poor, the children were poor. Even the butler was poor.'"

"Uh huh," responded H.J. "You told me that several times during our years together."

"Not all jokes are funny."

"I've noticed."

"Some go beyond funny to profound. You could switch this one, make the kid from right here in Westport."

Picking up a breadstick, she took a small crunching bite. "Ninety nine clop clop," she reminded him.

"That's an old joke, too." He sat up in his chair.

"We're already pretty certain it—"

"Hush," he requested. "Sure, it's an ancient joke and it runs like this—Who goes ninety nine clop clop?"

She waited a few seconds. "And the answer is?"

"A centipede with a wooden leg."

Her mouth turned down in disappointment. "That's it?"

After making a gratified chuckling sound, he said, "I don't have as many gags stored in my mind as, say, Henny Youngman, but I can still dredge up—"

"Yes, you've done admirably," she conceded. "Thing is, what the hell does it mean?"

He allowed himself to slump a bit. "Well, the dying message was for you not me," he said. "It should mean something to you. Centipede with a wooden leg?"

"Are you absolutely certain, Ben, this is the right joke?"

"How many other payoffs to ninety nine clop clop can there be?"

"It isn't even funny."

"Maybe it'll turn out to be another profound one." He sipped his wine.

She took a deep breath, held it for a few seconds before exhaling. "Okay, people are gathered around us at the damn mall. Rick is anxious to tell me where the money is hidden but he doesn't want any innocent bystanders to know the location. He decides to—"

"I've been thinking, H.J., that maybe he wasn't telling you where to dig up your 5,000 bucks."

"What do you mean?"

"From what you told me about that conversation, it could be he was really trying to tell you where to find something that could lead to money." He rested both elbows on the checkered tablecloth. "Meaning that even if we solve this

particular riddle, you may not end up with cash in hand right
away."

"Whatever I find, it's got to be worth at least what he owed
me."

"But it could be drugs or—"

"Rick wasn't in the drug business, trust me. He did some
sleazy things but drugs wasn't one of his sidelines."

"Have all your lovers since the divorce been on the sleazy
side?"

"Only a few. I do, though, tend to fall for one now and
then." She toasted him with her glass. "As witness our
marriage."

"Here I am helping you to find—"

"Actually Rick had a nice side. At first anyway," she said.
"When I started dating him, he took me across to Long
Island a couple of times—on the ferry."

"Say, that is nice. Only a prince of good fellows would—"

"We visited some old show business friends of his, at a
place called the Coldport Actors' Retirement Home."

"Whoa now. Did any of them happen to have a wooden
leg."

H.J. thought about that. "Nary a one, no," she answered
with a shake of her head.

"Had any of them played one legged parts?"

"How so?"

"You know, Long John Silver or—"

"If any of them had, they didn't mention it." She started
to reach again for her wine glass, then stopped. "Wooden
legs. I know who has wooden legs."

"Who?"

"It has to be—"

"Have the lady and gentleman made up their minds?"
The waiter had come shuffling up to their table.

"Give us another five minutes," requested Ben.

Tugging a large gold pocket watch out of his waistcoat,
the waiter laughed. "Romance. Slows everybody down."

"This is more commerce than romance," said Ben as the
waiter took his leave. "Go on, H.J."

"A dummy, of course."

"A store dummy or. . . . No, you mean a ventriloquist dummy."

She nodded. "There was a man there, old, about eighty at least. Probably you've heard of him, since he was supposedly big on radio about fifty years ago. McAuliffe. Bert McAuliffe."

Ben straightened up. "Sure, that's it. McAuliffe's dummy. Don't you remember is name?"

"I should, because he introduced me to the darn thing. Keeps it in a trunk at the foot of his bed. But I don't recall, no."

"Buggsy. Buggsy is the dummy's name. Sure, McAuliffe and Buggsy. Used to have their own show back in the early 1940s."

"Buggsy . . . bugs. And a centipede is a bug sort of, right?"

"Got to be. That's what Rick Dell was attempting to get across to you," said Ben with certainty. "Would have been simpler if he'd just said, 'I stashed something important in the wooden leg of McAuliffe's dummy.' But then—"

"He didn't want to do that, because somebody in the crowd might've heard and understood."

Ben tapped his fingers on the table. "All right, H.J., we seem to have cracked the message. This would be an excellent time to contact the police."

"No, not yet."

"Dell was murdered, your cottage was—"

"I don't want to drag poor ailing Mr. McAuliffe into this mess. He's in even worse shape than our waiter," she said. "No, I'll go over to Long Island tomorrow, find out exactly what is hidden in— "

"I'd better go along."

"Don't feel you have to look after me."

"We're not exactly friends any longer, but I'm still interested in your welfare. I'd hate to see you get murdered on a ferry boat or in an old folks home."

"Won't tagging along with me screw up your work?"

"I have to tape some radio spots for a new dog food the

Forman & McCay Agency is introducing. That's not until next Tuesday morning. Until then I'm free."

"What are you playing?"

"On the commercials?"

"Yes."

He glanced away. "A bowl of gravy."

"I suppose Dustin Hoffman turned them down, so—"

"Although you've never accepted the fact, Helen Joanne, I can do a better bowl of dog food gravy than Hoffman, or the late Olivier for that matter. The dialogue between me and the starving St. Bernard brought tears to the eyes of the jaded account executives during rehearsal the other day."

"Well, I guess I've no right to criticize you. After all, I sold out, too. Painting halfwit covers for trashy—"

"I haven't sold out. I always wanted to be a voice man," he said. "Mel Blanc, rest his soul, was my boyhood idol. So I happen to be doing exactly what I—"

"Pretty soon now the kitchen is going to close up tight," the waiter returned to announce. "If you can stop the romance talk long enough to give me your orders, I'll appreciate it."

H.J. smiled up at him. "I know exactly what I want," she said.

"Interesting," murmured Ben as he guided the car around another curve in the dark, quirky lane.

H.J. was sitting with her arms folded, staring out at the thin, fragile mist that was drifting down the roadway toward them. "What is?"

"I'm starting to get lower back pains."

"Oh, you always get those when you drive."

"But I haven't had a single pain lately. Not, come to think of it, in three years."

"Meaning that I'm the true cause of yet another of your multitude of problems?"

"Hey, I'm not blaming anyone. Merely commenting on a fascinating fact."

"If you think information about your backside is fascinating, I can see why you've been relegated to dating bimbos like Candy. What's her . . . wrong turn."

"Beg pardon?"

"You just turned onto the wrong road."

"No, I didn't. Fiddler's Lane leads right to your road."

"I'm off *Old* Fiddler's Lane."

"Ah," he remarked. He slowed the car, scanning the road for a place to turn around.

"Of course, we could park right around here and then trudge down through the brush, brambles, and trees. That'd take us to the rear of my cottage," said H.J. "That would probably, though, put too much of a strain on your ailing back."

"How come you live in such a dinky cottage, by the way? All the money you're allegedly making from compromising your talent ought to allow you to live in something a mite larger than a potting shed."

"Well, I prefer to invest my money wisely rather than dumping it into flashy pink mansions and—"

"Invest it in Rick Dell and other sound financial institutions, you mean?" He swung the car into a wide gravel driveway that apparently led to a far off house hidden by the trees and the darkness.

"Hold it a sec, Ben."

He hit the brake, leaving his car halfway backed out of the drive. "Something wrong?"

"Look back along the road, over yonder."

He twisted in his seat, squinting to look out the rear window. "Give me a hint about what I'm supposed to be seeing."

"There's a car parked back there, off the road and in among the brush. A Mercedes I think."

"Probably just a romantic couple."

"No, when we passed it I noticed . . . Yes, there it is again. See?"

"Looks like the beam of a flashlight, few feet from the rear of the car."

"I spotted it as we were driving by," she said. "Someone

just slipped clear of that car and is going to head downhill through the maples."

"Might just be somebody with car trouble."

"If you're having car trouble, you don't hide your damn car in the underbrush, Ben. You don't go sneaking through the woods to peek in my back windows."

"You think whoever it is with that flashlight is heading for your house?"

"Well, there is some precedent for that. They broke into my place once already tonight, remember." H.J. yanked open his glove compartment, poked a hand into it. "Don't you even have a flashlight?"

"Nope."

"Okay, all right. Here, take these matches." She produced a book of matches from her purse. "First thing to do is scoot over there and take down the license number."

"Actually the first thing to do, H.J., is to go call the law. If this is another break-in attempt, we—"

"I don't want to deal with the police yet. Not until I find out more about what those goons are looking for."

"We already know they're after something they're willing to torture and kill for."

"Jesus, never mind." She eased the door open and, before he could lunge across and grab hold of her, ducked out into the misty night.

▽

4

THE HEADLIGHTS OF THE Mercedes suddenly blossomed down the road, just as Ben was stepping clear of his car. The prowler must have heard H.J. approaching and decided to get away from there.

Ben started running along the dark road to catch up with his erstwhile wife. Just then the parked Mercedes came completely to life, motor roaring. It shot free of its hiding place amidst the trees. When it hit the road, the headlight beams caught the figure of H.J. between them.

She was about three hundred yards in front of the oncoming car, illuminated by the harsh white light.

Ben yelled, "Get off the road!" and started running faster.

H.J. seemed unable to move, halting there in the middle of the road. The black car was heading straight at her, picking up speed.

Sprinting, Ben reached her. He grabbed her, one arm snapping around her slim waist and the other hand clutching her shoulder. Staggering and stumbling, he rushed her toward the side of the misty road. The Mercedes went rushing by, like a harsh night wind.

Ben, tangled up with H.J., went falling into the brush at the roadside. The two of them rolled and tumbled until they thumped into a tree trunk

"Ease off," complained H.J., "you're jabbing me in the ribs." She wriggled free of him.

"Bastard almost got us." He shook his head, sucking in a couple of deep breaths.

"Did you get a look at him?"

"Nope, didn't get the chance." He pushed himself up to a kneeling position. "I was concentrating on saving your ass—and mine."

"Yes, thanks. I appreciate that." She was on her feet, bending to offer him a hand up. "And you didn't, I suppose, think to catch his license number as he whizzed by?"

Ignoring her proffered help, Ben got himself upright. "Now that you mention it, H.J., no, I didn't."

"Can't be helped I guess." She started hiking, limping very slightly, back toward his car. "Sure would've helped, though, if you had."

Ben followed, making a low growling sound now and then but not trusting himself to speak.

Hands behind her back, H.J. was scanning the book titles on one of his living room shelves. "Listen, I can phone my sister over in Westchester," she was saying. "I can stay there just as well as here."

"If these guys know where you live, they may also know you have a sister." He was crouched in front of his fireplace, arranging three small logs on the grating. "Nope, you'll be safer here than at Betty's."

"They might also, whoever they are, be aware that I have an ex- husband right here in Brimstone."

"That's less likely." He struck a match. "We haven't been officially married for three years, and you're using your own name again. Driving over here from your place, I made sure we weren't tailed."

"Kindling," she said, moving along to study another shelf. "Eh?"

"You never put enough kindling under the damn logs. That poor fire's just going to sputter for awhile and then die."

"There's a rule for situations like this," he told her,

standing up and away from the sputtering fire. "One never criticizes one's benefactors. That's part of English common law and dates back to about the middle of the—"

"You've got over a hundred diet books."

"Seven of them actually."

"They haven't," she observed, turning to eye him up and down, "helped much. You're even pudgier now than during our days together."

"I am, yes. Because in those grim days—called by most historians the Bleak Decade—I worried a lot more than I do now." He settled into a black armchair and watched the fireplace. "Worry and anguish are a great aid to shedding weight. I figure if you hadn't had all those affairs you did during our marriage, I'd have ended up weighing around three hundred pounds. But the Grief Diet you put me on kept me relatively svelte and trim, thus—"

"Why don't we have a truce?" she suggested, coming over to sit in a chair facing his. "We won't squabble at all while we're working together on this case. I'll simply ignore your obesity. I'll hide the goosebumps I'm getting because your fire is so anemic. I'll even—"

"Six and a half pounds overweight, Helen Joanne, isn't technically known as obesity. Nor is . . . okay, a truce. You quit first."

She smiled sweetly, spread her hands wide. "I have—not another bit of bickering will pass my lips. Honest."

"All right then," he said, "let's talk about this case of yours."

"Of ours."

"I've been thinking about all that's happened tonight," he began, trying to ignore the fact that his fire had ceased burning and was now only smoldering. "You say Rick Dell wasn't involved in drug dealing."

"That's one of the few things about him I'm sure of." Leaving his chair, she knelt in front of the fireplace.

"The thing is, it has to be something that involves more than just a few thousand dollars. Prowlers who drive around in expensive imported cars don't bother with paltry sums."

"I know what you're getting at, Ben, but it doesn't *have* to be something illegal." She slid the firescreen aside, and added fresh kindling under the logs.

"I think it does," he persisted. "Dell was bragging about big money coming in, but he sure wasn't on the brink of having his own HBO comedy special or starring in a television sitcom." Ben held up his left hand, fingers spread wide. "Which leaves, my dear Watson, the following possibilities for—"

"Don't do your Basil Rathbone voice just now."

"Oops, sorry. Didn't realize I'd slipped into that." Clearing his throat, he continued. "We'll list some of the other obvious possibilities. One, Dell swiped something from somebody. Something fairly valuable and relative small. Could be gems, cash, gold, bonds and so on. Two, he has some incriminating evidence against someone. That could be in the form of letters diaries, audio cassettes, video tapes, photographs. Three, he—"

"Ben, it could really just be something as innocent as gambling winnings." She touched a match to the rebuilt fire. "Or family money he'd come into somehow."

"Was he a gambler?"

"Sure, that's how the loansharks got him on their client list in the first place." Giving a nod of satisfaction as the fire commenced blazing, she returned to her chair.

"A gambler who loses all the time isn't likely to have a satchel full of money lying around."

"It only takes one big win to wipe out a lot of—"

"Sure, that's what most gamblers think. But it ain't necessarily true, daughter."

"Gabby Hayes."

"Right, used to be one of your favorites." He stood up and resumed his own voice. "You have got to accept the fact that this loot you're so anxious to track down is a by-product of something crooked."

She sighed and let herself slump in the chair. "Well, maybe you're right," she admitted. "I'll go over to Long Island tomorrow, though, since I do want to satisfy myself about what's hidden in Buggsy's hollow leg. There's no reason, however, for your coming along. I brought this on myself and you needn't get further tangled up in it."

"I already promised I'd go to the old actors home with you," he reminded her. "Once we find out the dummy's secret, we go to the cops. Agreed?"

She looked up at him, a bit sadly. Nodding, she answered, "Yes, you're absolutely right. That's the smartest course of action, Ben."

He got up, yawned once. "Want a cup of cocoa before turning in?"

"Nothing, thanks." She got to her feet, stretching. "Been a very rough day. Which room is mine?"

"If you'll just walk this way, mum," he invited, shifting into his sinister Karloff butler voice.

"It's going to be strange," she commented as she followed him up the staircase. "Sleeping under the same roof with you again, but in a separate bed."

Stopping, he glanced over his shoulder. "Right now, H.J., I think that's the best idea."

"Separate but equal," she said, smiling. "Yes, that is best."

He hesitated a few seconds before resuming his ascent.

$\triangledown$

5

BEN WAS AWAKE THE next morning and still entirely alone in his big brass bed, when the phone on his nightstand started ringing. He hadn't slept especially well, mostly because he'd had the suspicion that H.J. was going to wander in during the night with an excuse for leaving her room down the hall and sharing his bed. That hadn't happened, but he wasn't sure if that was good or bad.

She was as attractive as ever to him—at least physically. But starting up a relationship with her again was about as wise as having a couple of martinis on your way home from an AA meeting.

He answered the telephone on the third ring. "Hello."

"Ben Spanner, please."

"Speaking."

"Ben, old buddy, this is Les Beaujack at Lenzer, Moon & Lombard. I've been thinking about you lately and . . . Say, I didn't wake you up, did I? My wife always tells me I have an awful habit of calling people at the crack of dawn."

Ben sat up in bed, brushed at his hair with his free hand. "No, that's okay, Les. I've been up since . . ." He squinted at the bedside clock, noting that it was 8:40. "Been up and around since eight."

Beaujack, a vice president at the ad agency, did most of the hiring of voice talent for commercials. "You know, old buddy, I'm feeling damn stupid," he confessed. "Here we've been busting our collective ass trying to come up with the right man to play an English muffin on our new My Man Chumley radio spots—and I never even thought of you until late last night."

"Bloody shame, old man," said Ben, drifting into his James Mason voice. "Because I can do seventeen different British voices, don't you know. I'm jolly well certain that if I come in to read for your people, you'll—"

"Save the sales pitch, old buddy, since you won't have to audition at all," the advertising executive assured him. "You've got the job if you want it. I still, you know, remember that impressive job you did as the baby's bottom on the DynaDiaper commercial a couple years ago. Don't know why we haven't been using you more often. One reason, I suppose, is that you've been so damn busy of late. I'd better ask you right now if you're free tomorrow at two. We're, as usual, running about a week late on taping these things. Can you make it?"

"Two tomorrow afternoon, huh?" He glanced up at the buff colored ceiling high above him. "I'm flipping through my appointment book, Les. Nope, that's clear with me. I'll phone Elsie and have her talk to you about fees and contracts and such."

"Elsie Macklin," said Beaujack without a trace of enthusiasm. "Very aggressive little agent. Sure, tell her to get in touch. Meantime, old buddy, I'll be Fed-Exing you copies of the scripts."

"Okay, that'll be fine."

"We'll be expecting you at the agency in Manhattan tomorrow at two. And, listen, if this session goes well—as I'm damn certain it will—there'll be a lot more work for you. See you." He hung up.

Ben put down the phone and swung out of bed. "Fame and fortune continue to rain down on the personable, if a bit pudgy, Ben Spanner," he said aloud in his pompous anchorman voice. "He, according to latest reports, remains the same lovable chap he always was."

Ben trotted down across the dew-stained half acre of green lawn that fronted his home. After checking inside his bright silvery mailbox, he crouched and began scanning the underbrush around the box pole. After a moment he spotted his morning copy of the *Brimstone Pilot* lying among some plants that might be weeds.

Seating himself on the large decorative rock next to his drive, he began leafing through the newspaper. On page 5 he located the story—*Murder at the Mall*. After glancing back at his pink house, where H.J. was apparently still sound asleep, he began to read the account.

Rick Dell was indeed dead and gone. He'd been beaten and tortured, but the apparent cause of death was several knife wounds in the chest. He'd parked his car on an upper level lot and come into the mall. The police had no suspects at the moment, nor a motive. They were, however, extremely anxious to locate and question a witness who they believed might be involved in some way. She was a young woman described as "a stunning redhaired beauty."

Ben glanced toward his house again. "Stunning? Stunning?" he mused in his Sylvester the Cat voice. "Yes, I suppose you could say she is."

"You'll get piles sitting on cold stone like that."

"Good, since I've always wanted to have piles. But my parents claimed we were too poor to afford them." He stood up, grinned, then sat down again. "Morning, Joe."

Joe Sankowitz was a lean, dark man of about forty, decked out this morning in a faded grey running suit. A successful magazine cartoonist, he lived a mile and three-quarters downhill from Ben. "Want to join me for the rest of my five mile run?"

"No, actually I'd rather sit here and brood."

His friend studied him. "You look as though you've been up most of the night. Trouble plaguing you?"

Ben answered, "Plague is an apt word. Yeah, I feel pretty much like some great incurable pestilence has commenced sweeping across me."

"Can you give me the details in two minutes or less? I don't like to halt my running longer than that," said Sankowitz. "Or do you want to have lunch and tell me then?"

"By noon I'll be in Long Island."

"That bad, huh?" Sankowitz sat down beside him on the big rock. "Okay, so tell me now."

"It all began last night while I was in my kitchen contemplating chicken curry."

"I told you you ought to become a vegetarian."

"Anyhow, this is what happened . . ." He gave Sankowitz, one of the few friends he could confide just about anything to, a fairly thorough account of the unexpected reappearance of H.J. Mavity in his life, including what H.J. had told him about the death of Rick Dell, the dying message, the attempt to run them down with a Mercedes, and assorted other details.

Sankowitz stood up at the end of the account, massaging his left knee thoughtfully. Finally he said, "Do you want some advice?"

"I'm afraid it's too late for advice."

"Your first go-round with H.J.—ten years that one lasted, right?—that encounter caused you considerable grief," the cartoonist reminded him. "It's been my experience—and keep in mind you're talking to a man who's on his third wife and his twenty-second or twenty-third mistress—it's been my experience that resuming relations with a lady who caused you grief in the past in almost always guaranteed to cause you grief in the present."

"Yeah, I've been thinking along similar lines, Joe. But the problem is that . . . Oops."

The front door of the house had opened and H.J., dressed in a sedate grey suit, appeared. She waved at them, pointed at her wristwatch, pantomimed that it was time for breakfast and then a trip across the Long Island Sound.

"A gifted mime," observed Sankowitz. "And she is sort of stunning." Smiling sympathetically at Ben, he resumed his running.

$\triangledown$

6

THE LATE MORNING AIR was warm and clear; the husky white ferry boat was moving smoothly across the calm blue waters of the Sound.

Ben and H.J. were sharing a white bench on the open upper deck of the boat. There were about forty or so other passengers on deck, some of them sitting on the rows of benches, others at the railings.

"How about that guy over there with the tweed cap?" asked H.J. close to his ear.

Casually he turned to take a look at the man at the nearby railing. "Naw, he's with that fat lady."

"He's been watching us. I was afraid he might be a thug."

"He's been watching you actually. Maybe you shouldn't sit with your legs crossed like that."

"Jesus, Ben, I look absolutely prim in this outfit."

"Prim yet stunning."

"I didn't write that halfwit newspaper story."

"I'm nearly certain," he told her, "nobody followed us from my place to Bridgeport, or onto this boat."

Shivering slightly, she took hold of his arm. "Maybe I am getting sort of paranoid over this mess. Seeing potential crooks everywhere."

"Crooks quit wearing tweed caps in about 1940."

She gave a small, fretful sigh. "I'm glad you didn't let me down," she said, tightening the pressure on his arm. "I really don't think I could have made this damn trip all on my own." "Neither one of us has to go through with it, H.J. We can forget Buggsy, have lunch in Port Jefferson and catch the next boat back."

"No, I want to go at least as far as visiting McAuliffe and his dummy."

He leaned back, watching a scatter of bright white gulls circle high up in the morning sky.

H.J. inquired, "By the way, who was it that phoned early this morning? Candy perhaps?"

"I doubt I'll be hearing from her for a spell," he answered. "No, it was Les Beaujack. He's a VP at the Lenzer, Moon & Lombard Ad Agency and they want me for some My Man Chumley radio spots."

"Is that good?"

"Sure, since LM&L is one of the top advertising agencies. The Chumley account alone currently bills about $75,000,000 a year." He nodded, smiling. "They'll pay me a handsome fee—or at least a goodlooking one."

"Lenzer, Moon & Lombard," she said slowly, frowning thoughtfully. "Trinity Winters works for them, doesn't she?"

"Yes. She appears in all the television commercials and print ads for *Crazed* perfume." He switched to a sultry voice. "'I'm crazed with love . . . and in love with *Crazed*.'"

"Rick dated her."

"Rick Dell dated one of the top actress/models in New York?"

"For a while. I don't have all the sleazy details, but he flaunted her name to me more than once."

"He was seeing you and Trinity Winters at the same time?"

"Apparently."

"I'm impressed. Two stunning women simultaneously."

"Screw you," she remarked, letting go of his arm. "You still don't appreciate what an attractive person I am. That's why, during the seemingly endless years we were married, you undervalued just about everything about me."

"Our truce," he reminded.

"Well, you started it this time." H.J. uncrossed her legs, recrossed them. "Is it kind of strange, do you think, that the same agency that uses Rick's ladyfriend is also anxious to hire you?"

"Just a coincidence, H.J. I mean, if he'd been dating a woman who was an editor at Bantam Books and they offered you a cover, it wouldn't mean—"

"Yes, I suppose it is only a coincidence."

"LM&L has two dozen major advertising accounts, which means they hire a lot of talent each and every day," he said. "And I've worked for Beaujack before. So it isn't as though this were the first time they called me in to do some voice work."

"What did you do for them before?"

"Oh, just a voice for an animated cartoon spot."

"What product? Maybe I saw it."

"I doubt it's something you'd pay much attention to. It's DynaDiapers and—"

"Oh, that's the one where the little baby's rear end carries on a conversation with the paper diaper. They have a witty discussion about how ordinary paper diapers can cause itching and such. That one?"

"That's it." He looked out to sea.

"Which voice were you?"

"I played the rough, red baby bottom."

Laughing quietly, she took hold of his arm again. "That was a very cute voice," she said. "And very appropriate casting."

He worked free of her, stood and crossed the mildly swaying deck to the rail. The boat was drawing close to Long Island.

"Turn left just before the crest of this hill," instructed H.J.

Hunched slightly, Ben was behind the wheel of his car. The auto had traveled across the Sound on the ferry with them. "Nobody is trailing us," he assured her yet again. "You don't have to sit all scrunched up like that."

"It's best to take no chances." Knees tucked under her, she was keeping watch of the street behind them.

He executed the left turn. "I noticed a wide assortment of restaurants in Port Jefferson, during the brief time we were there."

"Tourist traps."

"Even so, we could've stopped for lunch."

"We'll eat after we see the ventriloquist."

The street they were driving down pointed toward the small harbor about a mile away, and was lined with trees and large old houses. Two and three story wooden ones, some trimmed in intricate gingerbread, sitting on quarter- and half-acre lots.

"There are probably even some dandy seafood places right here in Coldport."

H.J. untangled her long legs, settled into a new position on the passenger seat and frowned at him. "You're not going to distract or dissuade me, or any combination of the above," she told him firmly. "I'm going to talk to McAuliffe *and* I'm going to dismantle his damn dummy if need be."

"I've been thinking again about Rick Dell," he said. "They treated him pretty rough."

"I already know that, since he died right on top of me."

"If you get hold of whatever it was he had then they're sure as hell going to treat you rough, too."

"That's one of the risks, sure. Turn right after we pass that godawful mustard-colored saltbox house."

Ben did and they entered a cul-de-sac. At its end rose a narrow three story Victorian house, still vaguely white and rich with carved trimming, spires and cupolas. The sea wind had been working at it for over a century, rubbing away much of the paint, twisting the multitude of dark shutters askew, trying to pull the rusted weathercock from its high perch.

The wide front yard consisted of foot-high grass in which lurked a cast-iron elk, the remains of a tandem bicycle, a marble fountain topped by a tottering sea nymph, the weatherbeaten and possibly female figurehead off a sailing ship, and the ramshackle skeleton of a small gazebo.

"That's the Coldport Actors Retirement Home." H.J. gestured at it.

"I figured as much." He parked a few dozen feet from the sprung wrought-iron front gate.

"Let me do the talking." She left the car, gracefully and swiftly.

"Same ground rules as our marriage." He followed at a less enthusiastic pace than hers.

"You can be a sourball at times."

They started up through the overgrown lawn, following the remains of a path made of cracked and disordered flagstones. H.J. hurried up the swayback front steps, poking at the doorbell with a forefinger.

Far off inside the giant old house a buzzer made a faint choking sound. After a moment footsteps could be heard. The oaken door rattled, creaked, swung open inward.

"Well, my goodness, it's Helen. Nice to see you, dear, though under the circumstances, you'll excuse me if I'm not my usual jolly self." The manager of the home, a tall, plump woman of about seventy had opened the door. She had fluffy hair the color of brand new cotton and wore a pale green pantsuit.

H.J. smiled, studying the woman's face. "What circumstances, Mrs. Farber?"

"Oh, I thought that was why you were here, hon." She reached out of the house to pat H.J. on the elbow. "You and your other boyfriend used to visit him. It's poor Mr. McAuliffe."

Ben guessed, "He's dead?"

"He's dead," confirmed Mrs. Farber.

$\triangledown$

7

"Natural causes?" asked H.J. from the fat, flowered armchair.

"Why, yes, hon." Mrs. Farber set her cup on the claw-footed coffee table in front of her and gave the young woman a puzzled look. "Yes, he passed away in his sleep two days ago, poor man. That's me back in my Hollywood days, Mr. Spanner."

Ben was making a slow circuit of the cluttered living room, scanning the dozens of framed photos on the walls. "And that's George Givot and Isabel Jewell with you on the soundstage."

The manager chuckled. "You're the first person in years to recognize either one of them."

"Givot was a voice man on the side."

"Oh, are you in—"

"McAuliffe," put in H.J., recrossing her legs. "What exactly did he die of, Mrs. Farber?"

"Mostly just old age, Helen." She sighed, touched a knuckle to the corner of her right eye. "I was the one, you know, who found him. He was in his room up on the second floor, stretched out on his bed. He looked very peaceful and you might also have thought he was just taking a nap, except you can usually tell when someone's dead. His heart simply gave out, according to Dr. Weinberg."

Ben stopped in front of another large glossy photograph. "Here's McAuliffe," he said, tapping it.

The late ventriloquist, a heavyset blond man in a tuxedo, was sitting with his back to a dressing room mirror. Sharing the picture was a scatter of dummies.

"He wasn't an especially handsome man, but he was extremely likeable," observed the manager of the home. "Very kind to one and all with never—"

"Had he had many visitors lately?" asked H.J.

"Besides your other boyfriend, no. Except for his cousin. He had a cousin who lives over in Smithtown. As a matter of fact, that's who's paying for the funeral and all."

"Has anybody been to visit in the past few days?"

"No, dear, not even his cousin. If you know somebody's going to die, why, I guess you make an effort to see them one last time. But in this case, it was a complete—"

"I have a . . ." H.J. shifted in the chair, twisting her hands together in lap. "Well, it's rather a sentimental request I guess." She lowered her eyes, studying her hands. "But may I, please, take one last look at Buggsy?"

Mrs. Farber's sigh was deeper than the last one. "Oh, Buggsy isn't here anymore either, hon," she said. "No, he's going to be buried with Mr. McAuliffe. That was the poor man's wish."

Descending the front steps, H.J. briefly drooped. "Shit," she muttered, "I hate setbacks."

"I've noticed that."

"Damn." She paused on the cracked pathway to kick out angrily at the high grass. "Ow."

"What now?"

"I don't know. I stubbed my damn toe on something hiding in the weeds."

Bending, he parted the grass and weeds. "Appears to be what's left of a ceramic troll."

"Well, screw him." She resumed walking, arms stiff at her sides, hobbling a bit.

"We seem to have come to a dead end in our quest."

Just short of the dangling iron gate she halted abruptly, pivoting around to face Ben. "The hell we have," she told him evenly. "We're going to that funeral parlor Mrs. Farber mentioned—The Teenie Weenie Chapel in the Swamp or whatever the heck they call themselves."

"The Wee Chapel in the Glen Funeral Home," he provided. "Listen, don't think I'm being nonsupportive, but I draw the line at grave robbing."

"It's not grave robbing if the body is still above the ground. At the moment, Ben, McAuliffe is still lying in state."

"Even so, Helen Joanne, I think any kind of ghoulish activity is going to get us in deep trouble," he said. "Let's keep in mind, too, that we're on Long Island and not over in more liberal Connecticut. The penalties for bodysnatching are likely to be more severe over here."

"Dummysnatching can't be all that serious." Giving him a thorough scowl, she pushed through the gateway. "And keep in mind that . . . Oh, good afternoon. How are you?" She halted on the sidewalk, smiling.

A tall gaunt man in a venerable black suit was approaching the home. "Ah, my day is made," he informed her, bowing deeply. "Always a pleasure to encounter you, Miss Mavity."

"Same here, Marvelo."

"Here's but a small token of my esteem." From out his left sleeve popped a large bouquet of flowers.

They were cloth blooms, faded and frayed. Accepting them with a smile, H.J. pressed them to her breasts. "Thank you."

"And for your companion." A large peppermint stick appeared in Marvelo's right hand.

"Thanks, but I'm trying to quit."

The magician waved and the candy was gone. "I'm the Great Marvelo, sir—and you?"

"Ben Spanner."

"Ah, Miss Mavity's erstwhile husband. She's mentioned you on her previous visits to our little seaside hideaway. I've enjoyed your voice work on several commercials, in spite of some nitwit copy."

"Thanks. I remember seeing you on television when I was a kid."

"That indeed dates me." Marvelo took H.J.'s hand. "I was saddened to hear of Rick Dell's death, my dear, which I just read of in our local library's copy of this morning's newspaper." He tilted his head in Ben's direction. "I presume it's permitted to discuss a departed rival in front of you."

"I'm not in the running in that contest anyway."

H.J. said, "I understand Rick visited Mr. McAuliffe here by himself a couple of weeks ago. At least Mrs. Farber thinks so."

"McAuliffe is gone, too. I'd hate to think, considering my advanced years, that these things actually do go in threes."

"Did he, though, Marvelo?"

"He did, my dear, to be sure. Yes, Rick, looking very furtive and secretive—although, now that I think of it, he always looked that way. Something to do with his eyes being a mite too close together. Yes, he called on McAuliffe about two weeks since. Although my room is next to his, I didn't hear what they chatted about. I'm not above eavesdropping, but this time they spoke in very low tones. Even a water glass against the wall didn't help." He bowed again to H.J., deftly taking back his bouquet and hiding it away again. "Now I must go inside and catch my favorite soap opera. Nice to meet you in person, sir." Nodding at Ben, he started up the path to the house.

"Pizza," commented H.J. as she shifted impatiently on her side of the green booth, "never before struck me as the sort of food one savored."

"We've only been sitting in this place about eleven minutes and they only served us six minutes ago." He returned to slicing his wedge of mushroom pizza with knife and fork. "Relax."

"You're also the only person I know who eats pizza with a fork." She wiped at her palm with her crumpled checkered napkin. "Everyone else on the face of the Earth grabs it with their hand."

"I had a real high class upbringing, sister," he said in his Dead End Kid voice.

"Could you perhaps speed it up? I'm all finished and I would like to get over to the Little Chapel in the Ditch before sundown. We shouldn't even have stopped for lunch now."

"Missing meals isn't good for you." He chewed a bite of pizza, slowly. "And eating too fast causes stress."

"Eating fast doesn't hurt anybody. The whole damn country is devoted to wolfing down their food as rapidly as they can. My Man Chumley, for whom you'll be prostituting your talent tomorrow, boasts that they'll serve you in under two minutes or refund your— "

"Let me change the subject." He cut himself another small bite of pizza. "What do you say to our heading back to Port Jeff and hopping aboard the first available ferry for home?"

"What I say is no."

"Suppose—despite what Mrs. Farber says Dr. Weinberg told her— suppose McAuliffe was murdered, too?"

"At first, when she told us he was dead, I suspected that's what did happen," admitted H.J. "But then I used my powers of reason. See, McAuliffe died way before Rick did. And there is no reason to believe anybody knew two or three days ago that he was hiding something valuable for Rick. They probably still don't know that."

"Be that as it may, the idea of stealing Buggsy out of the coffin makes me uneasy."

"Ben, it isn't even, technically, stealing at all. Because Rick wanted me to have whatever it is he stashed in Buggsy's hollow leg. I mean, his reciting all that clop clop stuff in the Eastport Mall is practically a living will."

Ben said, "Things look to be getting increasingly complicated and dangerous."

"Finish your damn pizza," she advised.

$\triangledown$

8

THE FOYER OF THE funeral parlor smelled of flowers and furniture polish. The pink fountain at the center of the small oval room wasn't functioning properly and every few seconds a spurt of scented water shot up almost to the domed, pale green ceiling. Weak, forlorn, organ music was drifting out of two small dangling speakers.

A very old man in a wrinkled black suit was slumped, arms dangling and eyes shut, in one of the three straightback chairs that lined the far wall. A net shopping bag beside his chair had slumped, too, and spilled three oranges and a tin of deviled ham onto the hardwood flooring.

Tugging at Ben's arm, H.J. led him over to the announcement board on the wall to their right. "C'mon, kick up your pace," she urged in an exasperated whisper. "We're almost to our goal."

"We're almost into the hoosegow for violating a tomb."

"That only applies to Egypt, when you go break into a pyramid." She scanned the listings in white plastic lettering on the board. "There he is—McAuliffe, Reposing Room 3. They didn't give Buggsy any billing."

He leaned closer to her. "Let's go home. I can loan you the $5000."

"It's always a bad mistake to borrow money from a former

42

mate." She shook her head. "Besides, Ben, I really am caught up in the mystery now."

Saying nothing further, he accompanied her down a pale green hallway. She hesitated in the arched doorway to the reposing room. "I can't, from here, see who's in the coffin."

Easing around her, Ben crossed the maroon carpeting and halted beside the metal stand that supported the polished wood coffin. There were no mourners in the small room, the five rows of darkwood benches were empty. Arranged behind the coffin were six small floral wreaths on wooden legs. "This is the right one," he said.

Gingerly, she came into the room to join him. "I should've brought some flowers."

"Custom doesn't require grave robbers to do that."

"It really is McAuliffe?" She was watching her feet, not the occupant of the coffin.

"Appears to be, judging from my childhood memories and from that photo I saw back at the home."

Very slowly, and uneasily, she raised her head, stood on tiptoe and chanced a quick glance. "Oh, Jesus—I don't like to view bodies."

"You should be getting accustomed by now."

"Where's little Buggsy?"

Ben pointed. "Right over there."

The dummy's freckled face was visible on the far side of the coffin, wedged in next to the dead ventriloquist's right side, his red hair bright against the white satin lining.

H.J., fists clenching, forced herself to take a more careful look into the coffin. "Yes, that's Buggsy sure enough," she said. "He looks dead, too."

"Let's leave him be, Helen Joanne, and head for—"

"No, I've come this far and I intend to carry this through. Can you tug him out of there, Ben?"

"Might be easier to just reach in there and—"

"But Buggsy's legs are hidden by the lower half of the coffin lid," she said. "No, you're going to have to get hold of the little guy by his armpits and give him a good hefty tug."

"That's what *you* are going to have to do. I'm only an accessory, not the perpetrator."

"Honestly, you can be such a geek at times." Nudging him aside, she stepped closer to the coffin.

"Ah, I'm very glad to see this."

H.J. stopped still, then brought her forefinger up to her nose, sniffling. When she turned to face the newcomer to the room, she seemed to be crying. "It's so sad," she managed to say.

"He's had so few visitors, which is why I'm delighted to find you two here paying your respects." The man was in his forties, small, freshshaven, smelling of flowers and furniture polish. He wore a grey suit and a grey tie. "I'm Lynn Gerstenkorn, one of the partners in the Wee Chapel," he explained as he approached them. With a sad smile he handed Ben an embossed business card. "Should you ever need our services." He smiled even more sadly as he gave H.J. a card.

"My husband and I were dear friends of Mr. McAuliffe," she explained, sniffling while she dropped the card into her black purse. "And of little Buggsy, too."

"Let me, now you've mentioned him, ask you something." Gerstenkorn rubbed at his temples, then rubbed his hands together. "Does the dummy look—how shall I put it? Does he look tastefully laid out?"

"Very much so," responded H.J. "Don't you think so, dear?"

"Yes, yeah. He looks very natural. You'd almost think he was alive."

"We debated long and loud, my partners and I, as to whether or not it was good taste to allow the dummy to share the coffin," said the funeral director. "There's also the question of provoking unwanted levity. Still, it was Mr. McAuliffe's wish, and in his day, so.I've been led to understand, he and the dummy were a wellknown team."

"You've arranged everything quite beautifully," H.J. assured him. "Now, I wonder if my husband and I might be alone here to pay our last respects to them both."

"To be sure, certainly. I'll simply go sit down over there in the last row," said Gerstenkorn. "This, you know, is my favorite of our six minichapels. I always bring myself here at day's end for a period of quiet meditation."

H.J. asked, "How long a period?"

"Oh, usually a half hour."

Near to Ben's ear she said, "We'll have to come back later, damn it." Moving back, she smiled sweetly at the funeral director. "Why don't you, Mr. Gerstenkorn, show the flowers and their cards to my husband. I want to go freshen up before we leave."

"Flowers?" said Ben, watching her start down the aisle alone.

"Yes, you know how interested you are in that sort of thing. Kind of flowers, sentiments expressed, who from and so on."

"I fear there aren't as many floral tributes as one might have expected for a performer of Mr. McAuliffe's supposed status at onetime," said Gerstenkorn apologetically. "Do let me show them to you nonetheless."

"That would be," said Ben, "very nice."

A few minutes shy of midnight a light, misty rain started to fall. H.J. gave Ben a poke in the ribs. "The place's been empty for a half hour. We can make our move."

Yawning, he sat up a bit straighter on the car seat and peered down across the weedy hillside field toward the Wee Chapel in the Glen Funeral Home. It sat a quarter of a mile below the wooded area where they'd been parked for the past few hours. "What you're contemplating is called breaking and entering."

"We're not going to break in," she said, reaching up to flip the switch on the overhead light so that it wouldn't flash to life when she opened the door. "I already told you that, while you were chatting with Mr. Gerstenkorn this afternoon, I slipped that folded up business card of his in a side door so that it wouldn't close completely."

"There's still the question of illegal entry."

"Well, a funeral chapel is pretty damn close to being a church, and you can enter a church anytime you want." Turning the handle, she inched the door open. "That's known as the law of sanctuary and it's been in effect for hundreds of years."

"Looting a coffin, on the other hand, is still frowned on by the majority of the world's faiths." Yawning twice more, scratching at his lower ribs, he stumbled out into the new rain. "Suppose there's a burglar alarm?"

"There isn't. I made sure of that this afternoon." She strode across the wet sidewalk and entered the grassy field. Stuck in her purse was the flashlight she'd bought that afternoon. "The cops who patrol this area won't roll by again for another twenty-two minutes."

He followed her. "You logged their car every time it passed down there?"

"I'm fairly efficient, a fact that you never fully appreciated."

"You sure used to manage your affairs efficiently—"

"We better go the rest of the way in silence, to be on the safe side."

"Folks," he said in his sincere testimonial voice, "I went from respected actor to detested ghoul in just 24 hours. You can, too."

"Hush up."

The rain drizzled on Ben, insinuating itself down his collar and under his cuffs. There was a musty, earthy odor rising up from the weedy ground.

A single light showed at the front of the slantroofed chapel, illuminating a few of its imitation stained glass windows. H.J. made her way along the shadowy rear of the building and then around to the far side. She slowed, then stopped beside a wooden door. "Here's the one we want." Reaching out, she took hold of the knob to turn it slowly and carefully.

The door opened inward silently. The wadded up business card hit the hardwood floor with a faint tick. She hesitated and then, like someone balanced on the edge of a high board, took a deep breath and plunged ahead.

Ben slipped into the dark corridor behind H.J. and shut the door at his back.

"Here, you use this." She slapped the flash into his palm.

He snapped it on. "Minichapel 3 is this way."

H.J. took hold of his arm and they moved ahead, following the yellowish beam of the brand new flashlight.

The night rain made faint pattering noises on the shingled roof. The shadows in the hall gave off the familiar flowers and polish smell, with the scent of some sort of harsh chemical added.

At the entrance to the small chapel where McAuliffe and his dummy lay, H.J. took back the flash and shot the beam in the direction of the coffin stand.

"Oh, shit," she remarked after a few seconds.

Buggsy was no longer sharing the coffin with the ventriloquist. He was now spread across the floor, ripped into several jagged pieces.

$\triangledown$

9

ON HER HANDS AND knees, making disgruntled noises, H.J. sifted through the remains of Buggsy. "No trace of anything," she said finally, resting on her heels. "Not that I know what the hell I'm hunting for anyway."

"Something small and valuable." Ben was crouched beside her, holding the flashlight on the fragments of the dummy.

"Well, it looks like the competition—whoever they are— beat us to the prize." She picked up one of the dummy's detached legs, started to tap it angrily against her thigh.

"Notice that somebody took a knife to Buggsy and used it pretty enthusiastically." He played the beam around, pointing at the scattered parts.

"Damn, and we were so close, too," she said, tapping the little wooden leg against her leg. "They must've followed us over from Connecticut. Maybe that jerk with the cap *was* a—"

"Even if they followed us, which I don't think they did," he said, "that wouldn't have told them to rip up Buggsy to look in his hollow leg."

She said, "That's right, Ben. They couldn't have known about Buggsy unless . . . unless they made Rick talk some before he managed to get away from them."

"That's probably what happened, yeah."

"But then why did they search my house? If they already knew what they wanted was stashed inside this dummy."

Ben said, "Suppose what they're looking for is something that can be duplicated? Documents that can be photocopied, photographs, something like that."

"Sure, then they'd have to make certain not only of the originals, but of any copies Rick might've passed around."

He stood, tapping her shoulder. "We'd best depart before the law makes its next pass by here."

She got up, shaking her head. "I was sitting up there watching this damn funeral parlor for hours, while you were dozing, and I didn't see anybody suspicious," she said. "They must have broken in from the far side of the place as soon as the last employee went home."

He started for the doorway. "The people we're competing with have more experience in burglary than we do, H.J."

When they were halfway up the rainy hillside, she said, "Jesus, I brought this leg of Buggsy's along with me." She raised her hand to fling the thing off into the darkness, but then stopped. "Ben, this leg is sort of heavy, relatively speaking. Turn on the light for a second."

After glancing around, he clicked the flash on. "What do you mean?"

Rolling up the tatter of checkered pants leg that was still attached to the wooden limb, she rapped it with her knuckle. "This leg is solid wood, not hollow," she said. "You couldn't hide a damn thing in it—and I imagine the other leg must be the same. Hell, we misunderstood Rick's dying clue." Dropping the leg in her purse, she resumed climbing toward the car. "I feel exceedingly dumb."

He turned off the light, following her. After climbing a few paces in the night rain, he snapped his fingers. "Of course."

She scowled back over her shoulder. "Of course what?"

"The photo on the wall," he replied.

"You're sure about this?"

"Yes, there are two of them in the framed picture Mrs. Farber has on her living room wall."

"Two different Buggsys. I only met one, far as I know."

"He probably kept the extra one wrapped away in his trunk."

"Then the second one, the spare, must be the Buggsy with the hollow leg."

"It's worth checking."

"How come, by the way, you're willing to do this, Ben? Up until now you've been urging me to quit."

"It has something to do with seeing that dummy all slashed up at the funeral parlor."

"More evidence that these guys are vicious."

"It occurred to me that they might not give up on you even if they do find what they're hunting for."

"Meaning they might come back and rough me up—just for the fun of it?"

"Like the paint tubes, and Buggsy."

"So if we can get to the second Buggsy ahead of them—"

"Then we may have something to use to expose them. Once they're arrested, tossed in jail, they can't hurt you."

"That's touching, Ben, very thoughtful."

"They also won't be able to hurt me." He parked down the block from the old actors home.

The rain was heavier now, coming down enthusiastically. There was only one street light near, old and dim.

"I can sneak back in and search McAuliffe's room," H.J. offered. "I know the house, afterall, and in case there's some trouble, Mrs. Farber likes me."

"Nope, I'll do it. Have you finished drawing the floor plan?"

Working by the light of the flash, using a ballpoint pen on the back of a yellow garage bill she'd found in his glove compartment, she was sketching out the layout of the second floor of Mrs. Farber's establishment. "Okay, first you shinny up that fire escape on the right side of the house," she said. "Then you climb in the second floor window—it's always open a few inches because Mrs. Farber believes fresh air is important at night. Marvelo told me that during one of my visits here with Rick. McAuliffe's room is this one.

I've marked it with an X."

"That's a Z."

"I'm a professional artist. I guess I can draw a damn X when the occasion arises. Marvelo has the room right here."

"Judging from our conversation with him this afternoon, he likes to eavesdrop on what's going on around him."

"Right, so be extremely quiet while you're ransacking the trunk," she cautioned. "Mrs. Farber has a room at the back of the first floor someplace, so she isn't likely to hear anything."

Nodding, he took the flashlight from her and clicked it off. "Slide over into the driver's seat once I leave. In case we need to make a hurried getaway."

"You're trusting me to drive your car? In times gone by you were an extreme fussbudget about—"

"See you shortly." He eased out into the rainy 1 AM darkness. Ducking low, he hurried along the cracked side-walk. He felt as though he were doing an impression of Groucho Marx or possibly Chuck Berry.

There was a single dim light showing in the bow window of the living room, another up on the third floor. The rest of the big old Victorian house was dark.

Ben squeezed through the gap between sprung-iron gate and the fence. Crouching even lower, he started through the high, wet grass, trying to avoid trolls, elk, and other obstacles.

Suddenly he tripped over something and fell to his knees, losing his grip on the dark flashlight. A sharp pain started spreading from his left knee and he had the impression he'd bitten into his lower lip when he hit the ground. He stayed kneeling for a few seconds. Then, in his Lionel Barrymore voice, he quietly told himself, "You can walk again, lad. Get up and do it for old Dr. Gillespie."

Ben rose and then bent to start feeling at the ground for his lost light. He put his hand into something soggy he hoped was only a discarded mellon before he located the light and retrieved it. Then he went tottering ahead. A whooshing gust of wind threw extra rain onto him.

He had made it over to the side of the house and was

searching for the fire escape ladder when he walked into it. Taking hold of a rung with one hand, he looked upward. One story above him somebody was climbing rapidly down the same metal ladder.

10

PRESSING BACK AGAINST THE side of the house, with the rain slushing into his upturned face, Ben watched the dark figure descending. It was someone wearing black jeans, a navy blue pullover and a black skimask. As the person climbed quietly down toward the ground, something clacked against the metal ladder. That had to be, he was certain, Buggsy being carried down from McAuliffe's room.

Hidden in the shadows, he narrowed his eyes and tried to get a better look at what the burglar was making off with. As the dark figure dropped from the final rung to the wet ground, Ben caught a glimpse of Buggsy's red hair. The dummy was tucked up under the intruder's left arm.

Without pausing to contemplate what he was doing, Ben leaped forward and tackled the retreating figure around the lower legs. They both fell, skidding on the wet grass. Ben got a strong, and unexpected, whiff of a sultry floral perfume. He also, as they wrestled over the ground, realized he had tackled a woman.

Be that as it may, he grabbed for the dummy. He got a good grip on him, yanked, and succeeded in tugging him free of the masked woman. Thrusting Buggsy up under his own arm, he swung out with the flashlight in his other hand. It hit the woman in the midsection and she let go of him. He broke free and started running.

"Come back here with that!"

He kept running and made it almost to the flagstone path before he tripped. As he fell, the woman got to her knees and started shooting at him with a handgun.

When she saw the flash of the shots, H.J. sat upright, exclaimed, "Oh, my god!" and turned the key in the ignition. Releasing the brake, she stared out into the rainy night. The windshield was smeared with rain.

"Wipers," she said as she poked at various buttons to the right of the steering wheel. Nothing much happened, and the windshield wipers didn't start functioning.

"Well, screw them." She gunned Ben's car out of its space and into the street. Up ahead she saw somebody come hopping off the curb. She then remembered the headlights and found the right button on the second try.

The beams showed her Ben, with what looked to be Buggsy hugged to his chest, running toward her. Rising up out of the high grass several dozen feet behind him was a masked figure with a gun.

H.J. floored the gas pedal. Hunching low, she swung the car between Ben and the person with the gun. She hit the brake, flung the door open and yelled, "Get your ass in here, Ben!"

He dived inside as she slid clear of the driver's seat.

"We got him." Tossing the dummy in her lap, he grabbed the flapping door shut and sent the car barreling out of there. A parting shot slammed into the rear window, making a loud thunking, crackling noise and spreading cobwebby lace patterns all across the glass.

"Hell," said Ben, "how am I going to explain that to my insurance people?"

"I feel like I'm seducing a midget," observed H.J. as she tugged off Buggsy's checkered trousers. The car was now fifteen miles clear of the actors home and no one was following them.

Ben concentrated on driving, but glanced occasionally

over at the dummy resting across his ex-wife's lap. "Any sign of a secret compartment?"

She had the lit flashlight resting on the open door of the glove compartment, illuminating the dummy. "Yes, in his right leg here. A section seems to have been cut out and then glued back in. I don't suppose you've got a knife?"

"Nope, I don't. Until you came back into my life I didn't have any need for burglary tools or weapons."

"I'm not talking about a switchblade, Ben, but just a little dinky pocket knife so I can pry . . . Never mind." She commenced searching in her purse. "You're really certain that was a woman who swiped this from McAuliffe's room?"

"I am."

"Does that make sense?"

"As much as our breaking into a mortuary at midnight."

"No, I mean if this is a gang of loansharks we're competing with, it seems odd. Do they have female loansharks?"

"H.J., there's a lot more to this mess than Rick Dell's bad debts."

She located the nailfile she'd been hunting. "We've missed the last ferry boat across, haven't we?"

"By several hours."

"Want to stay over here in a motel someplace for tonight?"

"I want to get home, so I can be at my place by early morning. Beaujack's sending me copies of the scripts I'll need for the recording session this afternoon."

"It's a long drive, going all the way around the Sound back to Connecticut. You should get some sleep if you're going to be doing your funny voices."

"Even so."

She started working on the dummy's leg with her file. "C'mon, c'mon, pry loose," she urged. "Ah, here we go."

Ben took eyes off the night highway for a few seconds and saw her prying the section off the hollow wooden leg. "What's in there?"

She set the section of leg on the seat beside her. Nose wrinkling slightly, she lifted out something small and dark between thumb and forefinger. "This is it?"

"A roll of 35 millimeter film."

"I know but . . ." She closed her fingers slowly over the roll of film. "People are getting killed. People are getting tortured. We're being shot at. All for this?"

"Must be some important photos," he said. "And that just about proves that Rick Dell was a blackmailer."

"We don't know for certain that this contains blackmail photos." She brought her hand up nearer her face, opened it and studied the spool. "This could just as well be prints of a treasure map."

"It could be the plans for a new Disneyland in Yugoslavia," he said. "But I'm betting it's incriminating photos."

She tapped the undeveloped film on her left knee. "Darn, what an anticlimax."

"The point is, H.J., we've now found what we set out to find. It hasn't led to fame and fortune, but that's the way things go. As soon as we get home to Connecticut we'll turn this over to the police. That should get the hoods off our—"

"Bullshit."

"Beg pardon?"

"I'm not quitting this business until I know for sure what's on this roll of film," she told him. "If it is a map or a chart, I don't want a bunch of cops digging up my doubloons."

"So you want to get the pictures developed?"

"I surely do."

"Suppose it's thirty-six shots of a couple committing adultery in a motel? Fotomat's going to frown on—"

"We'll have to get them developed privately, schmuck," she said. "Hey, Joe Sankowitz is an amateur photographer, isn't he? He used to be when I knew him."

"Joe has his own darkroom, sure. But do you want to—"

"We can trust him."

"That's not it. I don't know if I want to involve a friend of mine in something crooked."

"Rick may've been crooked, Ben, but we're not."

After a few seconds he replied, "Okay, we'll stop by Joe's

when we get back to Brimstone."

She dropped the roll of film into her purse, deposited Buggsy on the floor. Placing a hand on Ben's arm, she sad, "Once we get a look at these pictures, I'll quit. I promise."

$\triangledown$

1 1

SANKOWITZ, LEFT EYE NARROWED, looked out at him through the narrow opening. "If you want to go running with me, you'll have to wait until ... But, no. Nobody would want to run in a business suit," he said, opening his front door wider. "Especially a business suit that's apparently been worn wrestling alligators in a swamp."

Ben blinked, then yawned. "Can you do me a favor, Joe?"

"More than likely. What?"

He shifted on the shaggy welcome mat, fished the roll of film out of his coat pocket. "Can you develop this for us?"

His friend looked from the film to his face. "Is this another chapter in your adventures with H.J.?"

"She's waiting in the car."

"You may recall my warning you about taking up again with ladies known to have futzed up your life," Sankowitz reminded him. "This is only a hasty diagnosis, mind you, but I'd guess that your life has been futzed up considerably during the past few hours."

"Somebody did try to shoot me," admitted Ben.

"See?"

"But we got away safely, and we're on the last phase of this business. Once we see what these pictures turn out to be H.J. is going to turn over everything to the police."

"Things are worse than I suspected, you're back to believing what she tells you. Remember the problems that she caused you during your—"

"Contact prints'll do," said Ben, yawning again. "I have to go into the city for that My Man Chumley job this afternoon, but do you think you can have them done by tonight?"

"I only have two finishes to do for *The New Yorker* and a color comp for a Westport ad agency." His friend took the film from his hand. "That's nowhere near as important as this obviously. You be home by eight?"

"I should, and if I'm not, H.J. can let you in."

"She's living with you again?"

"Just for now, because it's safer."

"I'd wish you good luck," said Sankowitz, "but I think it's too late for that."

Ben's agent had gotten him a leading role in a French farce, one of those plays where there are a half dozen doors that are continually opening and shutting. The problem for Ben was that whenever it was his turn to open a door, a corpse would come falling into the room. They weren't farce corpses either, but realistic ones splattered with blood and gore and sporting repulsive wounds. Taking the job had obviously been a mistake and he decided to quit.

He hadn't been aware that his agent had moved her offices, but here she was doing business in the cemetery on the old Universal set. Her cluttered desk was set up in the middle of a shadowy marble tomb, the fog machines were sending thick, chilly swirls of mist all around Elsie Macklin and her filing cabinets.

Somebody nudged Ben in the back, requesting him to hurry up and pay his last respects to the deceased.

He didn't especially feel like walking up to look into the open coffin, but he knew he'd be embarrassed if he didn't and he'd also disappoint the dozens of mourners who were lined up impatiently behind him. He stepped forward.

"Jesus, you weren't supposed to be home this early." H.J.

was lying naked in the coffin, making love to a naked redhaired midget.

"Close the damn lid, will you, buddy," requested the little man.

"I can't even trust you after you're dead, H.J."

Nope, this was definitely not the part for him. He'd have to get hold of Elsie right away to have her break the contract. Maybe if he shouted loudly enough his agent would hear him and do something.

He started yelling.

"Easy now, Ben."

"Anyway, farce isn't my strong . . . Hum?" He awoke to find his former wife, wearing a faded grey sweatshirt and jeans, sitting on the edge of his bed.

"Do you have nightmares often these days?"

"First one in three years." He sat up, shaking his head.

"You okay?" She put her hand against his forehead.

"Nothing more than a touch of black water fever, old girl," he replied in his Nigel Bruce voice. "No, I'm fine. What time is it?"

"Almost eleven, which is why I popped in to wake you. If you're going to catch the 12:33 from Westport, you'd better start getting ready."

He swung out of bed, then remembered he'd been sleeping in his shorts. "Oops, excuse me."

"I'm family, more or less."

Shrugging, he headed into the bathroom off his master bedroom. "Modern science tells us man can get by with four hours sleep."

"I apologize again for keeping you out all night, Ben," she said. "But I wasn't, you know, anticipating all the complications we ran into over there."

As he plugged in his electric razor, he studied his face in the mirror. "Gosh, I seem to have turned into Spanky McFarland overnight," he said. "I'll join you for coffee in the kitchen in a few minutes, H.J."

She came over to lean in the open doorway. "I do appreciate all the help you've been."

"It's okay, the new stresses you've brought into my dull routine will no doubt make a better person of me."

"But seriously." Leaning in, she kissed him on the cheek.

It was a pleasant spring afternoon and Ben didn't encounter anyone he knew on the train platform at Westport. The 12:33 pulled in at 12:31 and he got a window seat by himself. After opening the bottle of passion fruit-pineapple juice he'd bought at the small store across from the station, he took the three My Man Chumley scripts out of his attache case. Sipping the juice, he read over the scripts again. He was set to play, according to Les Beaujack's cover letter, the part of the First Muffin. A character described as "self-confident Cockney who's justifiably proud of being part of My Man Chumley's New $1.99 Kipper 'N' Muffin Bargain Breakfast."

Using his closed case as a lap table, Ben started marking his scripts with a red Pentel. He underlined all the speeches of the First Muffin. Then, trying out various voices and reading in a faint murmur, he checked the important words in each line of dialogue. The First Muffin carried on conversations with the Second Muffin, a snooty type, rejected by Chumley for lacking crispness, crunchiness and Honest-To-Blighty flavor.

Ben tried his Stanley Holloway voice, then blended in a touch of Roland Young.

"What is it this time?" The thickset graying conductor was standing in the aisle beside his seat.

"Hum?"

"You're going in to do another commercial, aren't you, Mr. Spanner?"

"Yeah, I am." Slipping his ticket out of his breast pocket, he handed it over. "I'm going to play a part in some My Man Chumley radio commercials."

"Do you know him?"

"Who?"

"Chumley—the guy who plays him, that is."

"That's Barry Kathkart. I've met him a few times over the years, but we aren't chums."

"Seems like a very warm, likeable person."

Ben looked out the window. "I hear he's not exactly that in real life."

Nodding, the conductor punched the ticket. "What are the chances of you getting a job like that for yourself? They not only use that guy on television and radio, but in magazines and newspapers, and even on all the cups and napkins. Just about everything but the toilet paper, but maybe they just haven't thought of that yet."

"I'm basically a voice man, not an in-front-of-the-camera actor."

"He must earn a lot of money."

"I've heard tell Kathkart makes more per year than a Metro North conductor," confided Ben. "Though I find it hard to believe any mere performer can do that well."

The conductor chuckled and moved on.

Ben returned to his scripts. He paused, leaned back, muttered the word "Blimey" several times in different voices. When he finally found the reading he was satisfied with, he returned to marking his lines.

He yawned twice, took another drink of juice. By concentrating on the commercials, he had hoped to keep his mind off H.J. This whole business he was now entangled in with her failed to cheer him.

She still looked great, though. Prettier than ever actually, if you were honest about it. But you had to keep in mind that there's more to a marriage than a wife who looks great. H.J. sure hadn't overcome her tendency to wander into trouble. This Rick Dell/ninety nine clop clop business was considerably more horrendous than her usual run of trouble, but it followed pretty much the same pattern he'd grown familiar with. She'd get into a screwed up situation, he'd feel obliged to help pull her out.

His life really had been different in the three years since they'd separated and divorced. He'd risen in his chosen profession, met new women, led a much less stressful life and a more content one, too.

A duller life, though. Yeah, and he had to admit that every so often he'd missed H.J.

Such thoughts were dangerous.

"Blimey," he said aloud.

$\triangledown$

12

HEAD LOW, MUMBLING HIS lines in the muffin voice he'd pretty nearly decided he'd go with, Ben stepped out of the elevator twenty six-floors above Third Avenue and 51st and walked smack into a very pretty blonde woman who was searching for something in her large scarlet purse. He became briefly entangled with her, executing a wobbly half turn before getting free.

"Asshole," remarked the blonde, elbowing him aside so that she might jump into the elevator just before its doors came hissing shut.

Backing across the thickly carpeted corridor, clutching his attache case to his chest, Ben stared at the closed silvery doors of the elevator. His nose wrinkled once as he muttered, "Same smell."

The young woman was the model Trinity Winters and she was wearing the same scent as the woman in the skimask with whom he'd wrestled on Long Island the night before.

The perfume must be *Crazed*. A popular one, worn probably by thousands of women. Except that Trinity Winters, judging by his quick go-round with her just now, also felt a lot like the masked female burglar.

That's a hell of a subjective judgement, though, based on a quick feel in the hall, he reminded himself.

Still, it was odd.

Everything is odd. Has been since you allowed H.J. to cross your threshold again. He noticed his watch, saw that the time was two minutes short of two and hurried into the Lenzer, Moon & Lombard reception room.

The place was large and white. The carpeting, the chairs, the reception desk, the platinum-haired receptionist were all shades of white. Three LM&L print ad proofs framed on the far wall provided the only trace of color, and they had wide white frames. Two of the ads were for the My Man Chumley account and featured full color shots of Barry Kathkart as the jovial butler.

Ben crossed over to the desk. "You know, I debated about wearing my white suit," he confided to the receptionist. "Now I'm sorry I didn't. I would've blended better."

She gave him a look that lacked sufficient warmth to be disdainful. "Yes?"

"Ben Spanner."

"Who?"

"Spanner. To see Les Beaujack."

"Oh, yes. If you'll take a seat, Mr. Beaujack will be ready for you very shortly."

An artist, who looked no more than twenty two, was the only other person waiting. He was slouched in one of the white chairs, his large black leather portfolio resting across his knees.

"Afternoon." Ben seated himself two chairs away.

"You're married to H.J. Mavity," said the shaggyheaded young man.

"Used to be."

"She's an interesting lady."

"She is, yes."

"Nice bone structure, too."

"You think so? I've never been quite satisfied with her ribs along this side."

"Facial bones I mean, speaking strictly from an artist's viewpoint," the young artist explained. "She isn't too terrible a painter either, if you like the trite, traditional paperback school."

"I do. In fact, I was always after my parents to send me to the trite, traditional paperback school. But they insisted on UCLA instead."

"Yeah, that's right." The artist folded his arms and turned away. "H.J. mentioned that you were an incurable wiseass."

Grinning, Ben opened his attache case and got out his scripts for further study. Eleven minutes later a white door to the rear of the receptionist flipped open and a middlesized, deeply tanned man of about forty looked out into the room. "Ben, old buddy, come on in," he invited. "We'll be taping right here in our in-house studio today."

"Hi, Les." Shutting the scripts away again, he got up and went over to shake hands with the advertising executive. "I think I've worked out the right voice for the—"

"I'm sure you have, which is why we hired you." He stepped back into the office area, holding the door. "Let me guide you through the labyrinth."

Just about everything on the other side of the door was white, too.

"By the way, I was glad to hear," said Beaujack over his shoulder, "that you and your lovely bride were back together again."

"Where'd you hear that?"

"Oh, around someplace. Isn't it so?"

"For the moment," admitted Ben after a few seconds. He followed Beaujack deeper into the agency.

The director up in the booth said, "My Man Chumley, Spot 32B, Take 7." He was a plump black man in his middle thirties. As he pointed at Ben through the glass now, he smiled with just a trace of weariness. The clock on the wall of the small studio showed that it was nearly four o'clock.

Ben leaned into his microphone and said, "Blimey, but I'm on top of the bloomin' world, I am."

The small, pale actor beside Ben said, "An' well yer should be, mate. You've been picked to be part of a blinkin' My Man—"

"Jesus H. Christ, aren't you ever going to read that line

right, jerk?" Barry Kathkart, standing at a microphone of his own, lowered his script to glare over at the small, pale actor.

"Barry, old buddy," said Beaujack from the booth, "Pierce sounds fine to us up here. Suppose we try to get all the way through his second commercial before we—"

"He sounds like a raving faggot," said the tall, broad actor.

"I am a faggot," said Pierce Gardener, "but that's no reason for you to keep—"

"Fellows," put in Ben, "I think Les has a splendid idea. Let's get a complete take on this thing and then see about what doctoring, if any, we—"

"If you want to kiss Les's ass, Spanner," suggested Kathkart, "do it elsewhere. I don't think your boyfriend's reading is right. And keep in mind that I'm really the one who has to be satisfied here. I sure as hell know what makes a good Chumley commercial. And let me tell you, brothers, this ain't it."

Ben said, "Granted you've sat in on some of the great muffin performances of the century, Barry. Even so, everybody else thinks Pierce is doing okay."

"Ah, the Sir John Gielgud of silly voices has spoken." Kathkart threw his script to the floor and went striding over to a far corner of the studio. "Les, fire both these assholes and get me two new muffins."

Ben said, "Come on, Barry, we're all professionals here and—"

"I'm telling you Pierce's reading isn't right, and yours isn't all that good either, Spanner." He poked a forefinger in Ben's direction and then at the booth. "Get him the hell out of here, Les."

"Hold it a minute, everybody," advised Beaujack. He came hurrying down out of the booth and into the room.

Giving Ben and Gardener a quick, rueful smile, he crossed over to Kathkart and started talking to him in a low murmuring voice.

"Have you worked with Kathkart before?" Gardener asked quietly.

"Never have, nope."

"I have—once before." He sighed, rolled up his script and rubbed it across his small chin. "I'm not coming across too swish, am I?"

"I've never heard an English muffin with more balls," Ben assured him.

"I would've liked to turn down this particular job, but I couldn't risk ticking Les off. They use me on a lot of other stuff."

". . . don't want to annoy *him*, remember?" drifted over from Les's murmured lecture to the big actor.

"Okay, okay," muttered Kathkart. "I forgot, Les, I lost my temper."

"This isn't Shakespeare, old buddy," reminded Beaujack in a louder voice. "Don't take it too seriously."

"All right, Les, but keep in mind that if *I* didn't take this goddamn job seriously the agency would have lost the Chumley account a long time ago." Kathkart came stomping back to his mike, squatted, grunted, and scooped up his discarded script with such force that he turned it into a ball of crumpled paper.

Beaujack tapped Ben's upper arm with his fist. "All your jobs for us won't be this rough," he promised. "Don't hold this against us."

"Right you are, guv," said Ben in his muffin voice, tugging at his forelock.

It was a few minutes shy of six-thirty in the evening when they finished recording the three My Man Chumley commercials.

1 3

THEY'D ENTERED BEN'S HOUSE at about five minutes shy of two that afternoon. Two of them, big men in dark windbreakers and skimasks. They had come down through a wooded area, pines and maples mostly, to the left of his house and slipped in by prying open the sliding glass doors of the living room.

They were very slick about breaking in, quiet, professional. But, even so, up in the guest bedroom H.J. heard them.

Her heart beat accelerated, but she didn't panic. Nor did she for a moment assume that they might just be friends or neighbors of Ben's dropping in for an afternoon cup of coffee.

I'd better get my butt out of here, she told herself, rising slowly and quietly off the bed where she'd been lying and reading through one of the business ledgers she'd dug up in Ben's study. He really was making over $200,000 a year now.

She dropped the blackbound book on the unmade bed, and took a deep breath. From the back of a wicker chair she grabbed her maroon sweater. She couldn't hear them downstairs anymore, but she sensed them.

She flatfooted over the window and, after breaking a thumbnail on the latch, urged it open, patiently and without noise. H.J. knew, from her earlier thorough casing of the house, that there was a slanting roof just outside this particular window. Poking her head cautiously out, she surveyed things. Nobody was stationed in front of the place, there was no sign of a car parked out on the road.

Taking another deep breath, she climbed out of the bedroom and made her way on hands and knees down across the shingled roof. She had the impression she heard someone coming up the stairs in the house she was abandoning. Not waiting to confirm that, she rolled over the edge of the roof and held onto it with both hands, dangling about ten feet above the side lawn.

Okay, Geronimo or whatever, she said to herself, letting go.

She hit hard, jangling her teeth. As she fell over, her right knee slammed into the ground. Making a sighing, unhappy sound, she scrambled to her feet and started running.

"I seem to be doing a hell of a lot of limping lately," she observed as she hobbled rapidly into the surrounding woodlands.

After a few minutes of running and stumbling, H.J. found a dark, shadowy spot rich in high, concealing brush. She hunkered down amidst the bushes with her back pressed against a tree trunk. Not once during the long uncomfortable hour that the men ransacked Ben's house did she consider calling the police.

H.J. was alone in the house, her auburn hair tied back with one of Ben's paisley ties, when Joe Sankowitz arrived a few minutes after eight that night. She opened the door holding a broom in her left hand. "You got them?"

Narrowing his left eye, Sankowitz inquired, "Am I interrupting your spring cleaning, Helen?"

"Come on in," she invited. "We had sort of an incident here this afternoon."

He followed her into the living room, tapping a large manilla envelope against his leg. "Jesus, what went on?"

"Housebreakers."

She had all the furniture put back pretty much where it

had been, but several hundred books, hardcover and paper-back, were scattered around the carpet in disorderly heaps.

"What did the police say about—"

"I didn't call them."

Sankowitz studied her face for a few silent seconds. "Meaning this is all part of the same general calamity that you've dragged Ben into?"

H.J. smiled. "He volunteered to help me out a little, Joe."

"Any idea who did this?"

"I got a distant glimpse of them when they took off," she replied, leaning her broom against the wall. "It was two big lunks with skimasks or maybe stocking masks over their thick heads."

"Where were you while they—"

"Hiding in the woods out there most of the time," she said. "I was here—upstairs—when they first broke in. But I jumped out a window and they didn't spot me."

"Me, I'd have run further than just these woods."

"You're into jogging."

"But they might have come hunting for you. You should have, Helen, put a few miles between you and them."

"No, I wanted to stay in the vicinity."

"Why?"

"Well, for one thing I wanted to be here when you showed up."

Sankowitz shook his head. "Ben isn't back from New York yet, huh?"

"Any minute, though. He phoned from Grand Central to tell me he was catching the 7:07."

"How'd he take the news of the breakin?"

"I didn't tell him. No use his worrying and fretting all the way home," she said. "Anyway, I've managed to get most of the damage cleaned up—except for all these damn books."

"I'll help you with those while we're waiting for Ben," offered the cartoonist.

"Before we do that, what about the film?"

Sankowitz walked away from her to sit on the sofa. "It turned out to be . . . very upsetting stuff." He placed the envelope on the cushion next to him and kept hold of it.

"But there were pictures, something came out?"

"Yes, there are nineteen shots."

She crossed over to him, undoing the necktie that was holding her hair. "Showing what?"

"I'm afraid it must be the aftermath of a killing."

She shook her head, causing her hair to fall to her shoulders. "Okay, let me see."

"I think we better wait until Ben gets here, because there are some very serious—"

"The pictures were, more or less, willed to me." Leaning closer, she snatched the envelope free of his grasp. She walked over to a thick black floor lamp.

"Helen, this all could be very—"

"Relax, Joe." She unfastened the clasp and slid out the cut up sheets of proofs and a glassine envelope of negatives. After scanning a few of the shots, she laughed. "Bingo."

$\triangledown$

14

B<small>EN WAS KISSED BY</small> H.J. soundly, on the mouth, seconds after he came through the doorway from the garage into the kitchen. "Yes?" he asked when it was over.

"Welcome home—wait till you see the pictures." She caught hold of his arm, tugging him into the hall leading to the living room. "Oh, and don't have a fit."

"What might I have a fit about? Is Joe here yet?"

"He's in the living room. But I meant because of the burglars."

He halted on the threshold. "We were visited by burglars?"

"I'm afraid so."

Sankowitz bounced up off the sofa. "Ben, I think you've got to call the cops in. What you're into is not a simple, funfilled treasure hunt. These guys—"

"Were you here, H.J., when it happened?"

"Only for a brief while, Ben." She took his attache case away from him, guided him to an armchair. "I cleaned up just about all the traces of—"

"Christ, they dumped every book I own.—"

"I haven't gotten around to the books yet."

"This is very scary stuff," said Sankowitz. "These guys broke in, they trashed your house and . . . If they'd caught

Helen they might have done her serious damage."

"I didn't get caught, though. And once they left, I—"

"What did you do?" Ben put his hand on her shoulder. "How'd you avoid them?"

"I was upstairs taking a nap. I heard them breaking in down here, lucky for me, and went right out a window. I slid down the roof and headed into the piney woods."

"Damn it, Helen Joanne, you could have been murdered. Or broken your neck."

"But I escaped, I survived," she pointed out, hugging herself and smiling.

"So far you've survived, but that's sure no guarantee that—"

"Ben, please. I really am not in the mood for one of your avuncular lectures just now." Walking over to the coffee table, she bent and gathered up the contact prints. "Hush up for a minute and take a look at these, will you."

"Make it a quick look," advised Sankowitz, sitting uneasily back down. "Then rush all these pictures over to the law."

Ben took the cut up proof sheet. "You really think . . . Holy shit!"

H.J. laughed and said, "Impressive, huh?"

The first shot showed two men carrying the body of a portly grayhaired man out the rear door of a colonial mansion. The man at the head end of the probable corpse was Barry Kathkart, looking nowhere near as amiable as he did when playing My Man Chumley. At the foot end, obviously struggling with the heavy body, was Les Beaujack.

"Beaujack and Kathkart," murmured Ben as he slowly scanned the rest of the sequence.

The pictures, taken at night and probably with some kind of zoom lens, showed the actor and the advertising executive lugging the body of the grayhaired man out of the mansion, down along a stretch of white graveled drive and then depositing it in the trunk of a Mercedes. In the final three shots you could make out a very unhappy Trinity Winters and a lean, sour-faced older man standing by and watching as the corpse was being stuffed into the trunk.

Perching on the arm of Ben's chair and crossing her legs, H.J. said, "I can identify everybody but the dead man and that old coot next to Trinity."

Ben said, "Actually we're not sure the guy they're lugging around is dead."

"Oh, so? You usually don't rush somebody to the emergency room in the trunk of your car."

"You're right," he agreed. "The fellow next to Trinity is Arthur Moon."

She pressed her hands together, smiling. "The CEO of Lenzer, Moon & Lombard?"

"That Arthur Moon, yes."

Sankowitz said, "You know, there's something familiar about the old gent they're carting off." He came over to take some of the photos away from Ben.

"Do you know him?"

The cartoonist's forehead acquired a few new wrinkles. "He's not a friend of mine, if that's what you man," he answered. "More like somebody I maybe met once—or saw on television years ago."

"He seems to be at least seventy." H.J. glanced hopefully at Sankowitz.

He gave a negative shake of his head. "I can't dredge up a name as yet. Could be it's only that he somewhat resembles my Uncle Herschell."

H.J. rubbed her fingers across the back of Ben's neck. "Do you realize what we've got pictures of?"

"A safe guess would be that this is the windup of a murder."

"That's not necessarily so," said Sankowitz from the sofa.

"What else," asked H.J. scornfully, "would it possibly be?"

"The man might simply have had a heart attack."

"If your Uncle Herschell dropped dead in your parlor," said H.J. impatiently, "would you haul him off to dump in a culvert? What I mean is, if you didn't have anything to do with his kicking off, you'd phone the police or the paramedics. And you'd sure as heck leave him lying where he fell."

"I would, sure," agreed Sankowitz. "Thing is, Helen, I'm not the spokesman for a multimedia, multimillion dollar food account. Nor, last time I checked, am I an important exec with a prestigious advertising agency. These people don't want any scandal."

"That part is right, they sure don't." She recrossed her legs, rubbing at her bare knee. "It's dead certain one of them killed this poor old duffer. To avoid any legal trouble or any scandal that would hurt the Chumley account, they decided to get rid of the body. Then they could pretend that none of them had a thing to do with sending him on to glory."

Ben tapped one of the small photos. "This, by the way, is Kathkart's place," he said. "We went to a party there one time years ago."

"You and me?" asked H.J.

"Us."

"I don't remember," she said. "But if this is Kathkart's house, he's likely the one who committed the murder."

"That doesn't necessarily follow."

"Sure, it does. Beaujack didn't drop over to Kathkart's to kill off one of his guests. It has to be Chumley who killed . . . Damn, I wish we knew the victim's name."

"I may come up with the name eventually." Sankowitz studied his share of the photos again. "There are other ways to find it out, though."

"Obituaries," suggested Ben.

"If he was well-known, yeah. We can assume that Helen's late chum took these pictures within the past couple of weeks, so we—"

"They are recent, because Trinity has her current hair style," said Ben.

"Okay, then you can definitely check recent obits."

"Suppose they dumped the body in the Sound in a gunnysack full of scrap metal?" H.J. left the chair arm to start pacing in a wide, lopsided circle. "There won't be any obituary in that case."

"But there still might be a missing persons notice of some sort."

"Be more likely that they'd dump the body a safe distance from Kathkart's place in Westport," suggested Ben. "And try to make it look as though the guy had met with an accident or been mugged."

H.J. halted and eyed her former husband. "Hey, how do you know about the present state of Trinity Winters's hair?"

He leaned back in his chair, letting the photos rest on his knee. "I hate to mention all this," he said. "But it occurred to me a few minutes ago that I didn't get my latest My Man Chumley role solely because of my impressive talent."

Snapping her fingers, H.J. said, "Beaujack wanted to get you out of the house, so he could have somebody come here and search it."

He nodded, tapping another photo. "This is probably the same Mercedes that tried to flatten us the other night," he said. "And it's probably Les Beaujack's car."

"So he saw you with me, figured you must be involved in all this mess."

"Or at least that I might know something about what Rick Dell was up to," said Ben. "Beaujack was very cordial to me today, but he did make a few remarks that seemed odd even at the time. Yep, I have to admit that he had ulterior motives for casting me as an English muffin."

"Was Trinity at the recording session, too?"

"Nope, she was hurrying out of the agency as I was arriving. We bumped into each other. She didn't seem to recognize me—but I'm near certain she's the masked woman who shot at me and tried to swipe Buggsy."

"Golly," remarked Sankowitz, "this is getting better than I dared hope. Gun toting models, hairbreadth escapes, all the—"

"Hush," H.J. interrupted.

Ben said, "Here's probably what happened—some night within the past week or so. Kathkart, who is known far and wide for not being the calmest and most even tempered of men, got into a situation that produced this elderly corpse. We don't know why yet, since we don't know who the dead man is. Let's see, Trinity was probably at Kathkart's for some—"

"Definitely was," cut in H.J. "She's been dating My Man Chumley, remember?"

"Allright, so probably Trinity was with him. The victim shows up for some reason, there's a fracas, Kathkart kills him—"

"Allegedly kills him," ammended Sankowitz.

"Allegedly my ass," said H.J.

"Kathkart realizes he's in big trouble. But—and this has to be the key to what happened—he also realizes that he's damn important to the ad agency. If he's arrested for murder—or even manslaughter—it screws up the whole and entire My Man Chumley account. He and the agency stand to lose millions of dollars, The Chumley image goes flooey and the client is—"

"They're very conservative, too," said H.J.

"Who?"

"The Walden Food Corporation, the folks who own My Man Chumley. Mom and the flag sort of people," she said. "If word got out that Chumley was slaughtering kindly old codgers, it would annoy them no end."

"Exactly. So Kathkart says to Beaujack, and possibly Moon as well—'Gee, I seem to have this corpse on my hands, fellas. Suppose you come over and help me get rid of it. Otherwise we all lose millions.' "

"A loyal ad man like Les Beaujack," said H.J., "would hop into his Mercedes and whiz over there with a shovel and a sack of quicklime."

"Could be you're a mite too cynical," suggested Sankowitz. "Not all advertising folks are crass and mercenary."

"Kathkart sure is, though," said Ben. "Les Beaujack, too. I don't think he'd have much of an ethical struggle over something like this. Not with all the money involved."

Sankowitz asked, "How'd Rick Dell fit into all this?"

H.J. answered, "He'd been dating Trinity off and on and he . . . Well, he had a habit of tailing his ladyfriends sometimes and snapping photos. Unbeknownst to them."

"That might indicate he tried blackmail before this," said

Ben. "Did he ever try photographing you?"

"Not to my knowledge, no. But he did confide in me that he'd done it with other ladies," she said. "There was jealousy involved, whether or not he also had blackmail in mind. I'd guess that he was out on one of his patrols, tailing Trinity and snapping pictures from a safe distance. Then all of a sudden a murder took place and he was close enough to get photographs of the mopping up operation. He may also have seen the victim going in to Kathkart's home and recognized him."

"Another thing I've been wondering," said Sankowitz. "How come Dell didn't develop these shots himself instead of hiding the undeveloped roll in the dummy?"

"That's another side effect of his lousy economic situation."

"How so, Helen?"

"Rick did a lot of amateur and semi-professional photography, but he never had a darkroom of his own. He usually shared the set up of a photographer friend of his over in Norwalk," she explained. "But when it got to the point where he was into this friend for around $2500 worth of supplies and equipment, the guy locked him out. That happened about two weeks ago and I imagine Rick didn't have access to another darkroom, not one he could trust with pictures like these. But since he'd been on the scene, he knew what he had seen and he obviously made his blackmail pitch without bothering to develop the stuff."

Sankowitz said, "You realize the consequences of all this? Kathkart and Beaujack, as well as Trinity Winters and old man Moon, are implicated in this murder and the death of Rick Dell."

"Of course," she said, nodding her head. "Initially I didn't think poor Rick was onto something this big, but, damn, this is really terrific. The whole My Man Chumley account is in jeopardy, the—"

"Whoa now." Ben put his hand on her wrist. "I don't like that glow that's starting up in your eyes."

She smiled at him. "No need to worry, Ben. I can get

excited about being involved in something like this, but I'm not dippy enough to think I can carry on where Rick left off." She stood up, brushing a wrinkle out of her skirt. "No sir, first thing in the morning you can escort me to your friends on the force. I'll tell all and we'll turn these pictures and the negatives over to them."

Ben said, "Great, that's the smart thing to do."

"Seconded," added Sankowitz.

$\triangledown$

15

"Do you always wear that?"

"Only on special occasions."

H.J. was seated on a raw-wood stool in Ben's big kitchen, watching him as he concentrated on a skillet on the front burner of the stove. "You never wore a candystriped apron while we were married."

"You never let me cook." He sprinkled a few more flakes of oregano into the sauce he was concocting.

"And now you actually do this sort of thing regularly—cook entire meals for yourself?"

"For myself and select guests."

"I never would have predicted your developing a domestic side, Ben." She rubbed at her knee with her forefinger.

He checked the pot of water next to the skillet. After tossing a few flakes of oregano into the boiling water, he took a handful of spaghetti out of one of the jars on the stoveside counter and introduced that into the pot. "For the first five or six months after we parted I relied on frozen food, restaurants and diners, and softhearted friends. Then I decided to try cooking from scratch. It started right after I did the voice for the Chef Pronzini Cooking School commercial spot. 'Anybody she can cook.' as the chef put it."

"Was that you on that commercial?"

"Yep."

"It was cute."

"I often am."

H.J. said, "That's not an especially large account is it?"

"Bills about $2,000,000 a year."

"Nothing, though, like the My Man Chumley account."

"Nope."

"What did you say they spend with the agency each year?"

He gave his bubbling spaghetti a quick stir, then bent to sniff at his sauce. "$75,000,000," he replied. "Which means LM&L's share is something like $15,000,000."

"Imagine making that off just one account every year."

"They won't be making that any longer," he reminded her. "They're going to lose the Chumley account fairly soon after we turn those photographs of Rick Dell's over to the police."

"The My Man Chumley restaurants are going to lose money, too. Sales will fall off."

"Initially, yeah. The fact that Chumley is apparently a murderer won't build up much positive publicity." He lowered the heat on the pasta.

She said, "I can see—not that it's right—but I can understand Rick's being tempted. With so many millions of dollars involved, millions that Lenzer, Moon & Lombard could go on making if they just got hold of the pictures. And Barry Kathkart must be pulling down a goodly sum, too."

"I've heard his take for playing Chumley is $1,250,000 a year."

"Rick probably asked them for what? A million bucks, would you guess?"

"At least. But keep in mind, Helen Joanne, that he didn't get even one buck. He just got killed."

"He made some mistakes obviously." She left the stool, went to a window and stared out into the night. "Either he set up some kind of preliminary meeting that went wrong— or he tipped his hand when he contacted that bunch to tell them he had something on them. Somehow they were able to identify him and find him, then they tortured him to get him to talk some."

"He must have told them about Buggsy, yeah."

She said, "But somehow Rick broke away from the goons that had him. This is rather a romantic notion in a way, especially for a schmuck like Rick—but he must have had it in his mind that he was supposed to meet me at the mall. Even in his dazed condition, dying and all, he clung to that idea and . . ." Her voice trailed off. "Poor guy."

"There's an obvious way they could have figured out who he was."

"Which is?"

"Suppose he telephoned Kathkart to make his initial pitch. Seems likely Kathkart would've taped the conversation."

"Suppose he did, what . . . Oh, certainly. If Trinity heard the tape, she'd recognize Rick's voice. Even if he tried to disguise it, he wasn't very good at voices."

"Did he do voices for you?"

"Sometimes."

"Where?"

"What do you mean?"

"At dinner, in the car, in bed?"

"Well, actually, Ben, in bed mostly," she answered. "Not that I especially enjoyed it, mind you, but Rick liked to do cartoon characters."

"Which ones?"

"Oh, I don't know. Well, mostly Bugs Bunny, Porky Pig and Tweety."

"Great, most of the Warner Brothers stable while in the sheets." He stirred the spaghetti and then the sauce. "Go seat yourself, dinner is about ready."

"Can't I help?"

"Not at all."

"You're miffed, aren't you? If you'd indicated, while we were living together, that you want to say, 'What's up, doc?' while we were having sex, I'd have been perfectly willing to go along with— "

"'I'd rather you didn't do those awful voices around the house all the time, Ben.'"

She smiled. "You don't do a very good me." She went into the dining room, lit the two candles at the table and sat down. "I didn't, keep in mind, do any of this with Rick while we were married. So there's actually no need to be jealous." She slipped her napkin out of the wooden ring, snapped it to unfurl it and dropped it across her lap. "Rick was sort of cute, though, when he went, 'That's all, folks,' after we'd—"

"Never mind." He came into the room, set a plate of pasta in front of her. He put the other plate at his place and, after shedding the apron, sat opposite her. "Wine?"

"Yes, please."

He picked up the previously uncorked bottle of chianti and filled her glass and his. "After all, as you pointed out, I have no reason to be concerned about all the affairs you had after we split," he said. "The ones you carried on before we separated, I could fret over, but these newer ones are none of my business."

"Ben, there was only one during all the time we were together," she said, looking directly at him. "And, truly, I'm sorry I ever slept with Guapo Garcia."

"What voices did he do in the sack?"

She took a slow sip of her wine. After setting the glass aside, she rested both elbows on the table. "I'm sorry about Guapo mostly because it eventually wrecked our marriage. I didn't intend for it to do that."

"Oh, really?"

"In fact, during these past few days . . . Well, hell, there's no need to bring that up."

"Bring what up?"

She said, "I've been realizing that I've missed you considerably, Ben. Most of the people I've met since we separated, most of the men anyway . . . they aren't much like you."

"Is that good or bad?"

"Listen, if you'll quit being so damned sulky, we might just try, for one night anyway, to recapture what we used to have."

"I thought we were recapturing that—bickering and arguing."

She rose up, came around to stand beside his chair. "Would you like to go to bed? Right now?"

He stood and instead of saying anything, put his arms around her and kissed her.

She said, "Would you . . . Do you remember, when we were first married and living in that converted bar in Redding, that you used to carry me up to bed?" She slipped an arm tentatively around his neck.

He considered for a few seconds. "I can still do that."

He did, lifting her gently off the floor and starting for the stairway. They were on the third step when she said, "Oops, we forgot something."

"Such as?"

"The pictures. We better not leave them sitting out on the coffee table all night."

He carried her into the living room. Leaning, she gathered up the contact prints and the manilla envelope.

Then he carried her up to the master bedroom.

The morning was splendid, judging by the portion of it that showed through the bedroom window. Clear and bright, with an assortment of cheerful birds singing in the trees.

Ben sat up, stretched, yawned, smiled. "Howsa bout some breakfast?" he inquired in his Chef Pronzini voice.

When the tangle of blankets next to him didn't respond, he narrowed his eyes and prodded it with his left hand. There was nobody under the mound.

"H.J.?" He left the bed and scanned the room.

Her clothes were no longer where she'd flung them last night on the far side of the bed.

Then he noticed light showing under the shut door of the bathroom. Barefooted, Ben went over and knocked, "H.J., you in there?"

No answer.

Opening the door, he stepped in. The large yellow and white room was empty. There was an open tube of toothpaste next to one of the twin sinks, squeezed near the top end the way H.J. persisted in doing. One of his hairbrushes had been moved, and he found a few auburn hairs clinging to the bristles. Traces of the quiet floral scent she wore still hung in the moist air.

She's probably down in the kitchen, he told himself. Or maybe out walking in the . . . Hey! The pictures.

He rushed back into the bedroom, going straight to his bureau. They'd deposited the contact prints and the negatives in the top lefthand drawer.

He yanked the drawer out so vigorously that it came completely free, twisting in his grasp and spilling most of its contents onto the carpet.

He squatted to examine what had fallen, even though he could already see that the pictures and the manilla envelope were gone. He left the drawer and his scattered socks and underwear lying on the floor.

"That nitwit. Jesus, she's going to try to blackmail those bastards on her own."

Locating the clothes he'd shed the night before, he hurried back into them. He tied his shoes as he hopped out into the upstairs hall.

"I've got to catch her before she does anything fatal."

He went down the steps two and three at a time.

While they were married H.J. had developed the habit of leaving messages on the dining room table. Maybe there'd be a note on his table this morning.

The plates from the uneaten dinner were there, the spaghetti cold and stiff, but there was no message. Ben grabbed his glass of wine, and gulped it down then doubletimed into the kitchen and the door leading down to the garage.

"Try her house first. Maybe she went there from here."

He pulled the door open, plunged through, stopped on the cement floor. "Oh, come on now. Shit."

His car wasn't there. H.J. must have taken that, too.

16

THE CAB DRIVER WAS a bearded man in his sixties, wearing a red mackinaw and a yachting cap. "What would you guess my real profession to be?" he inquired as he sent the vehicle rattling across town by way of back roads and winding rural lanes.

"Hum?" Ben was slightly hunched in the backseat, alternately gazing out into the bright morning and consulting his wristwatch. It was nearly 10 AM. He had no way of knowing how many hours ago H.J. had slipped away.

"Driving a hack is not my true calling."

"Ah," said Ben.

"So I was asking if you would care to hazard a guess as to my actual line of work. This present occupation you find me in being but a temporary lull in my career."

Ben said, "Sea captain?"

"That's interesting you should guess that. Several of my passengers have."

"Possibly it's your hat."

"Hell, I picked the lid up at a thrift shop in Westport. You can find most anything in Westport thrift shops. I bought a Chinese gong there once," said the whitebearded driver. "Take another guess, why don't you?"

If H.J. had been loose for several hours, there was probably not much chance of his catching up with her. Ben scowled at his watch again. "Give me a hint," he remembered to say.

"Well sir, I hate to do that. Because it would, see, mean that I don't look like a natural born example of what it is I am."

Rubbing his fingers across his palm Ben said, "Wait now, I'm starting to get something. Let me see. Yeah, that's it. I am getting a strong image of a horse . . . yes, a great white stallion. You're in the saddle, galloping across the plains of the Old West. What else am I getting a hint of? Yep, there's a faithful companion to you for many a long year. I am also getting . . . Yeah, you're wearing a mask and a white Stetson. And I think maybe silver bullets play a part in your profession. Am I at all warm?"

"Say, what the hell is wrong with you?"

"Eh?"

"Listen, I was just trying to pass the time pleasantly. There's no reason for you to razz me."

Ben said, "You mean you didn't used to be the Lone Ranger?"

"You know, I haul a lot of people around Fairfield County, rich and poor alike. Most of them respect me and few razz me." Making a grieved noise, he fell silent.

Ben looked at his watch.

This time there was a note. Ben found it on the front seat of his car, weighted down with his keys. The car itself he'd found parked halfway up H.J.'s short weedy drive. The message, printed in his ex-wife's personal mix of upper and lower case letters, read— *Thanks for the loan of the car. All is well, trust me. Will contact you soon. Love, H.J.*

He stood there in the sunshine, reunited with his car yet far from happy, holding the note in his hand. H.J. had printed it on the back of a gas station credit card receipt she'd borrowed from his glove compartment.

"I bet she's going to try it," he said to himself, shivering once. "That lunatic is going to attempt to get money out of Kathkart and Beaujack and the rest of them."

Unless he found her, cut her off before she made contact with anybody. Otherwise, she was almost certain to end up like Rick Dell.

Folding the note and sliding it into his hip pocket, he shut the car door and started along the doorway toward the garage. Maybe H.J.'s auto was still in there, which would mean she hadn't gone anywhere yet. He looked over at her small house, spotting no sign of life inside.

Now might be a dandy time to look up your contacts in the Brimstone police, he suggested to himself. Either Sergeant Kendig or Detective Ryerson. Probably Kendig would be the better bet, since he's a shade more liberal.

He looked in through the dusty window in the garage door, and let out a disappointed sigh. Her car was gone.

How liberal would a cop have to be, though, to condone what he and H.J. had been up to? Maybe if they'd been able to go to them this morning with the pictures in hand. Sure, with pictures to back up their story, their activities over on Long Island could have been downplayed.

"A little graverobbing, sarge, sure, and a touch of burglary. And there was some shooting in the streets. But, hey, it was all in a good cause and we have this evidence of a murder."

Absently he rubbed some of the dust away from the window with the heel of his hand. One of H.J.'s old suitcases, the one she'd taken that time they'd gone up to Cape Cod, was sprawled against the back wall.

Without the photographs, he couldn't prove a damn thing. Except maybe that he and H.J. had broken into a funeral parlor and that H.J. had fled the Eastport Mall just after Rick Dell expired.

And now, with the photos and the negatives in her possession, she was probably contemplating blackmail.

"How would the police react to my telling them I think my wife is about to start blackmailing somebody? Even cops I did fifteen minutes of comedy impressions for at a benefit show."

Not too favorably probably.

"Officers, my wife—make that my former wife—is planning to blackmail some very influential people. Could you guys, please, toss a net over her and keep her out of trouble? Don't arrest her or anything rough like that, because she means well and is just overly mercenary at times. She's a terrific person down deep and good looking, too, not to mention trustworthy and loyal."

Hell, if he went to the police now, all that would happen would be that they'd arrest H.J. Even if she showed them the photos Rick Dell had taken, they'd probably still lock her up and charge her with something. Plus which, he still wasn't absolutely certain she was dumb enough to go up against these people. It could be she was simply going to stay off by herself for a day or two and wrestle with her conscience. Away from him, so he wouldn't be able to argue with her.

"By tonight, though, if you haven't heard from her and haven't been able to find her then, damn it, you have to see the police. Even if that means her getting arrested."

He walked up the path to the house. It was unlikely she was in there, but he wanted to make sure. He was on the porch, taking hold of the doorknob, when a calm voice behind him said, "Just stay right there, if you would. Don't make any sudden moves."

$\triangledown$

17

VERY SLOWLY AND CAREFULLY Ben turned around. A pale blond man in a wrinkled tan suit was standing at the bottom of the steps watching him. He was just under six feet and just a few months from forty.

Ben said, "Morning, Ryerson."

"Well, Ben. I didn't recognize you from the back." Detective Ryerson smiled faintly. "But I guess this makes sense."

"Our running into each other?"

The policeman reached inside his coat, took out a fat canvas-covered notebook. "You used to be married to Helen Mavity," he said. "The fact is, I remembered seeing her picture the one time I was at your house. That's how I made a tentative identification."

Ben suffered a sudden chill. "Tentative identification," he managed to say. "Has something happened to her?"

"Not as far as I know." Ryerson flipped open the notebook. "Were you expecting otherwise?"

"It sounded as though you'd found her in some condition that made positive identification impossible."

"I haven't found the lady at all, though I'd like to. Is she at home?'

"I'm not exactly certain. I was going to knock."

"Do that," suggested the policeman.

Ben knocked. "What exactly are . . ."

The door had swung inward when he hit it and was now standing half open.

Ryerson stepped up onto the porch. "Miss Mavity, are you at home?" he inquired into the opening. There was no response from within the house. "You try calling her."

"H.J. It's me."

Continued silence.

Detective Ryerson pushed the door all the way open and waited, listening for a few seconds. Then he crossed the threshold. "Anybody home?"

Ben followed him in. "Again?" he murmured when he got a look at the living room.

The books he'd helped his onetime wife put back on the shelves were on the floor again, furniture was knocked over, a lamp was broken.

Ryerson scanned the disordered living room. "Why'd you say *again*?"

Ben swallowed. "H.J. was never much of a housekeeper and at first I thought she'd left her place in a mess again," he ad-libbed. "But I can see now there's been some sort of break-in."

"Are you and your wife getting back together?"

"We happened to run into each other again recently. She suggested I drop over sometime."

"And you picked this morning?"

"Happened to be passing by."

"That your car in the driveway?"

"Mine, yes."

"Engine's cold."

"She borrowed it earlier, and I actually stopped by now to pick it up."

"Where might she be at the moment?"

"Well, probably out in her own car."

"She's got a car, but she borrowed yours?"

"Hers was in the shop. She got it back, though, earlier this morning."

"How'd you get here?"

"Cab."

Ryerson nodded and took a sheet of folded paper from between the pages of his thick notebook. "This is Helen Mavity, isn't it?"

Ben unfolded the sheet. It was a fuzzy copy of a photograph of H.J. She was wearing jeans and a pullover sweater, staring down at a thin man who was kneeling on the mosaic flooring of the Eastport Mall. Dell hadn't been an especially good looking man. "Vague resemblance to her I suppose, but it's tough to tell with a picture that's this blurred."

The detective was starting into the hallway. "It's a copy made off the video tape from one of the mall security cameras. All the police departments in the county got copies of it and were asked if they could identify the woman," he explained. "I couldn't at first, but then I remembered seeing that picture of your wife."

"Ex-wife." He started after the policeman.

"That might change, though."

"You can loan somebody your car and not necessarily be thinking of remarrying her."

"Know the man in the picture?"

"Which one, the guy who's all bloody?"

"Yeah, that one."

"Nope."

"Him they identified. Name was Rick Dell."

"A thirdstring comic. I've heard of him, but didn't know him personally."

"So learning he's dead didn't move you to tears?"

"Not especially, no."

Ryerson went into H.J.'s bedroom. "When your wife—ex-wife— borrowed your car, Ben, she didn't happen to mention that a friend of hers had recently died in the Eastport mall?"

"No, she didn't." The closet door was open and he could see that the large skyblue suitcase he'd seen there the other night was now gone.

"The reason Rick Dell died was that somebody stuck a knife in him."

"That's right, I read about it in the paper."

Genuflecting, Ryerson checked under the bed. "You're right about her housekeeping. Flock of dustballs under here, along with some lingerie, Kleenex and a copy of . . . what is it? . . . *Passion in Manhattan*."

"She painted the cover."

"Did she?" The detective pulled out the paperback, stood up and studied the bright cover. "Woman in the nightgown here looks sort of like her."

"She sometimes uses herself as a model."

"Very nice painting, very attractive lady." He set the paperback book carefully atop the rumpled bedspread and stepped back into the hall.

"Are the police looking for the woman in the photo?"

"The Eastport police would like to talk to her."

"Was Rick Dell killed at the mall?"

"No, elsewhere. He only came to the mall to die." The detective stepped into the kitchen. "They went through this room, too."

The cupboards had been searched again, cans and cartons were strewn about the floor.

"Did she keep much jewelry or cash around the house?"

"I don't think so. H.J. isn't much for jewels. Money she likes, but that would be in her bank."

Nodding, the policeman moved along to the small, bright room that H.J. used as a studio. "Another self portrait," he observed, crossing over to the study the unfinished painting on the easel.

This room had been left pretty much alone, though someone had tossed a tube of vermillion paint on the floor and tromped on it. It had made an explosion of red across the straw rug.

"Did she mention to you if she'd had any earlier problems with burglars?"

"Not to me, no," answered Ben. "If she had had a problem, I'm sure she would have called the police."

"Any idea when she's due back home?"

"No, you never know with H.J."

"Everybody calls her H.J.?"

"Most of her friends."

"Did Rick Dell owe her money?"

"I'm not sure she even knew him."

"Since he died at her feet, it's a safe assumption she did."

Ben shrugged one shoulder and said nothing.

"One of the witnesses mentioned that H.J.—if it's her in the picture—that she asked Dell about money. 'Where's my $50,000?' is how it was reported to me."

"A tidy sum, even these days."

"As I say, that's what my colleagues on the Eastport police passed along to me," Ryerson said. "You wouldn't know if Dell or anybody else owed her that amount?"

"I'm not as convinced as you are that H.J. is the one in the picture. So it's just as likely that Dell owed money to an entirely different woman."

Reaching out, Ryerson retrieved the picture. He folded it and returned it to his book. "If you see her—when do you expect to be seeing her?"

"Later today probably."

"Mention that I'd like to talk to her. This isn't my case, but I like to help my colleagues out."

"I'll tell her."

"Also tell her to call me if she wants to report this break-in—or whatever it was."

Ben said, "I will."

"We can go now. Or did you want to stay here?"

"I'll go."

"Nice running into you again. Only last week somebody was saying how funny your impersonations were at that show."

"Thanks."

On the porch, after setting the lock, the detective pulled the door shut. "Anything else you'd care to talk about, Ben?"

"Nothing, not a thing."

He held out a hand. "See you then."

After shaking hands, Ben stood on the porch and watched Ryerson walk down the path. His car was parked just behind Ben's.

"I should have told him the truth," he said to himself. "And then let the police help look for her."

That might have led to their arresting H.J., though.

"Then I'm going to have to find her by myself—and soon."

$\triangledown$

1 8

Ben ARRIVED AT FAGIN'S Diner on the Post Road in Westport at a few minutes after one.

Fagin himself, a grim unshaven man of fifty-five was lurking in the doorway of the kitchen. Both his lumpy hands were hidden beneath his spattered white apron. "Too late for the luncheon special, Spanner," he grumbled.

"Darn, I wish now I hadn't run down that crippled newsboy in my haste to get there."

The proprietor sneered, turning away to make an offensive remark to a thin waitress.

Ben joined Sankowitz in a booth against the back wall. "What was the special?"

"Meat loaf—or a near approximation."

"That's almost always the special."

"Has been for the six years that we've been enjoying the sunny Fagin ambiance. Any luck on locating her?"

"No, none at all. I probably shouldn't even be taking time out to—"

"Starving isn't going to help you track Helen down. What have you tried?"

Ben slumped in his seat, resting an elbow on the table. "Been phoning people, including H.J.'s sister over in West-chester. All of them claim to have no idea where she is."

"Is the sister being truthful?"

"Hard to judge." Absently he picked up the one page menu. "Betsy has always ranked me three or four notches below Typhoid Mary on her list of favorite people."

"Who else did you call?"

"Couple of old friends of hers, and her art rep in New York." He shrugged. "Nobody's heard from her today."

"You'd expect she'd check in with the guy who's selling her work, since it involves money."

"I again made the mistake of approaching him as myself. H.J. must've told him at some time or other that our marriage was the inspiration for the *Texas Chainsaw Massacre* movies."

"What you have to do is bring in the police. You can tell them she's a probable missing person and—"

"Not yet."

"When you encountered your friend Ryerson this morning, Ben, that would have been a good time to—"

"I know, but I couldn't."

"Why?"

Ben shook his head slowly. "I had visions of their locking her up."

"Being locked up is better than being stretched out on a slab."

"Even if I did talk to Ryerson about this mess," Ben said, "I don't have any proof now. She made off with the photos *and* the negatives."

Clearing his throat, Sankowitz told him, "We have a couple of photos actually."

He sat up. "How'd that happen?"

"I made blowups of two of the shots of their lugging the old fellow to his penultimate resting place," the cartoonist confessed. "I told you I thought I recognized him, and I wanted to keep a picture to jog my memory."

"Have you succeeded in jogging it?"

"Not as yet, but I'm going to spend this afternoon over in the library going through the back issues of the *New York Times* for the past week or so," he said. "The thing is, you now have at least two pictures to show the police."

"If I don't track her down by nightfall," promised Ben, "then I'll do that."

"The people she's planning to hustle are dangerous."

"There are still some things I'm not sure about. For instance, Ryerson says it may be $50,000 that Dell owed her and not $5,000."

"How does he know that?"

"Somebody overheard her and Dell talking about the money at the mall."

"Be realistic, Ben. Helen wouldn't—probably couldn't—loan anyone a sum like that. It's more likely the witness heard wrong."

"There could be that kind of money involved if Dell was dealing drugs."

"No, Helen wouldn't fool around with anybody who—"

"This isn't a London coffee house set aside solely for conversation," called Fagin from across the diner. "Order something if you're planning to squat all day in one of my booths."

Ben told the unkempt owner, "I had my heart set on meat loaf."

"You can still have that, dummy, except that now it'll cost you $1.25 more."

"Done," said Ben.

"I'll have the same," said Sankowitz. "The meat loaf isn't as dismal as the stew."

"There's less alien life swimming around in it." Ben sat back. "Christ, maybe I am handling this all wrong. One of my real problems is I don't think I exactly trust her. I'm afraid she's more involved in whatever is going on than she admitted. If I get the police involved, H.J. could end up in jail."

"You have to decide whether you can afford to gamble that they won't kill her before you make up your mind—"

"She may phone me, too. That's another possibility. If she does, I can persuade her to drop the whole nitwit idea of blackmailing them."

"But she hasn't phoned you thus far, has she?"

"No, not according to my answering machine as of a half hour ago."

"Okay, try it your way. But keep in mind that I have the pictures on hand when you need them."

"Gravy?" hollered Fagin.

"No gravy," responded Ben.

"Gravy," requested Sankowitz.

"Fifty cents extra," reminded Fagin.

"No gravy," amended Sankowitz, picking up a folded copy of the *Westport Daily* from his seat. "Kathkart apparently isn't letting his conscience make a coward of him. At least he ain't hiding from the public eye."

Ben took the newspaper, turning to the story his friend had circled in red. "He's going to be making a personal appearance over in Westchester tonight."

"As the lovable Chumley."

" 'The new attractive My Man Chumley restaurant in Wolvertown, New York is the 1500th in the highly successful nationwide chain and there will be a gala celebration in connection with its opening,'" he read. "Imagine 1500 of those places blighting the nation."

"Imagine 1500 Fagin's."

"That would be worse, yeah. 'Also making a much-anticipated appearance will be glamorous high fashion model Trinity Winters.' Oy."

"All they need is Beaujack and Moon to have a full set of scoundrels."

"Les will probably be over there in the background someplace." Ben set the paper aside. "Possibly even Moon."

The thin waitress appeared with their lunch plates. "Act nonchalant," she advised in a whisper.

"We've been doing that," Sankowitz told her.

"I smuggled you some gravy, but don't let Fagin catch on."

"It'll be our secret," Sankowitz assured her.

The tiny red light on his answering machine was blinking

when he arrived home at a few minutes past two. Sprinting across his den, he poked the play button.

The machine cleared its throat.

"This is Elsie. Wepman & Corkis wants you to audition for a Skinny Minny commercial. You can do a Swedish meatball, can't you?"

"Yumping yimminy," he muttered impatiently, awaiting the next message.

"We have an important call for you but all our operators are busy right now. Please stay on the phone."

"I don't owe any creditors anything. Next."

A sultry aggrieved voice said, "This is Candy. Are you mad at me?"

"I'm indifferent."

There were no further messages.

"Shit," he observed when he realized that. "Why the hell don't you phone, H.J.?"

He sat on the edge of his desk, eyeing the phone. He twined his fingers together, untwined them, twined them again. Then, picking up one of the slips of paper from his desk, he punched out a number. After three rings a polite-sounding young woman answered, "Lester Salaman."

"I say," said Ben in a suave voice that blended the best elements of George Sanders and James Mason, "I do so hope you'll be able to help me, my dear."

"Possibly. What might I do for you, sir?"

"This is Edmund Yates here. Only going to be in your New York City for one more day, dash it all," he informed her. "I happen to be the Chief Art Director with Muse Books of London and I'm most eager to contact one of the gifted artists your Mr. Salaman represents."

"He's still out to lunch, but perhaps I might—"

"Jolly well hope so, my dear. We have in mind hiring this particular artist to paint the six initial covers for our forth-coming romance series," continued Ben. "Since this is an important new venture for Muse we intend to pay, as you clever Americans so delightfully put it, top dollar."

"Which of our artists are you interested in, Mr. Yates?"

"Deucedly talented young woman named Helen Joanne Mavity. Signs her work HJM."

There was no response.

"Are you there?" inquired Ben.

"Mr. Salaman ought to be back in the office no later than four. You can—"

"Typical American lunch hour, eh what?" He chuckled, throwing in a touch of Nigel Bruce. "The rub there is, my dear, that at four, don't you know, I'll be boarding a bally plane for my return to England."

"Oh, I thought you said—"

"Stated I was leaving today. Of course, it well may be the fee we have in mind to pay Ms. Mavity isn't that impressive to you affluent Yankees on this side of the Big Pond," he said. "Just a moment—I'm converting this from pounds in the old bean. Yes, I do believe I've got it right now. We can offer $15,000."

"For the entire six—"

"Dash it all, no. I mean $15,000 per paperback cover. That would be $90,000 for the entire bloody batch. If you'll excuse my rough language, my dear."

"Oh, certainly. The problem is, Mr. Yates, I don't think there's any way I can reach Mr. Salaman, since he wasn't sure which restaurant he and—"

"Actually, don't you know, it's the Mavity wench herself I'm beastly eager to have a bit of a chinwag with," he put in. "There are one or two very small points that must be cleared up with her personally. If she and I can reach an agreement on those, why then I'll be able to dash off the suitable contracts to your Mr. Salaman within hours of my return to Merrie England. It's our usual policy to include a draft for half the agreed upon amount—$45,000 in this case—when we post the contracts."

"Perhaps I could ask Miss Mavity your questions and get back to you. You see, she left instructions that she wasn't to—"

"Afraid not, my dear girl. It's imperative that I have these few words directly with her."

Another pause. "Well, she isn't at home today," said the perplexed secretary finally. "But she did phone in a temporary number just an hour or so ago. For emergency use."

Bingo! thought Ben. "Do pass it along like a dear girl," he urged.

"This is in Westchester County. That's in New York State. In a town named New Milman," she said. "There's an inn there called Victorian Village Lodge."

We spent a weekend there six years ago, said Ben to himself. "Sounds a jolly quaint little spot. The phone number is what?"

The young woman gave him the telephone number and the number of H.J.'s room. "You might mention to her, if you get hold of her," concluded the secretary, "that we considered this important enough to bother her with."

"I shall, my dear. Thank you ever so much. Tally ho."

Ben hung up, grinning. He picked the phone up again and punched out the inn number.

"Thank you for calling Victorian Village Lodge, a bit of nineteenth century tranquility amidst the hustle and bustle of modern living. My name is Angie, how may I help you?"

"This is Dr. Mackinson." he told her in his E.G. Marshall voice. "I have a message here that one of my patients—a Miss Helen J. Mavity—has been trying to reach me."

After a few seconds the woman replied, "I'm sorry, there's no one here by that name."

Ben said, "The room number I was given is 616."

"Oh, yes, she's registered as H.J. Spanner."

"Her married name I believe. Would you, please, connect me with her room."

"She's not in just now, doctor."

"Are you certain, young woman?"

"Yes, I saw her go out about an hour ago, and her key is still in the slot."

"Hmm," said Ben in a thoughtful, medical way. "Perhaps it would be best if you didn't mention I called, young woman. Yes, I don't want to upset Mrs. Spanner unduly in her present condition. I'll make it a point to telephone her again later in the day."

"Whatever you think best, doctor."

"Do you have any notion when she'll return to the inn?"

"I don't, sorry."

"Thank you anyway, you've been most helpful." After he put the phone down, he clapped his hands together. "Off we go to Victorian Village."

$\triangledown$

19

AT A FEW MINUTES after two H.J. had gone strolling. She'd left the inn, which looked like the mansion of some 1890s robber baron with questionable taste, to take a walk across Victorian Village. It covered five rolling acres and consisted of an eclectic main street some two blocks long with a collection of transplanted and refurbished last century buildings. Beyond that stretched fields and woodlands, a few antique barns, and a small white New England church sitting on the pinnacle of a low, gentle hill.

H.J., wearing a tan windbreaker, a checkered shirt, and jeans, had her purse held close to her side. Within it, in a separate envelope now, were the negatives of Rick Dell's photos. She'd attached strips of package tape to the envelope while she was back in her room.

The village hadn't changed much since she and Ben had been there five or so years before. It didn't look any older; everything seemed frozen in the nineteenth century yet well cared for. Among the restored buildings were a smalltown drug store with apothecary jars cluttering its window and a swinging-door saloon with a sign depicting a huge foaming 5¢ glass of beer sitting on the wooden sidewalk in front of it. There was also a darkwood general store with long-gone products lining its shelves and, as H.J. had anticipated, a narrow two story museum trimmed with gingerbread and painted a lively lemon yellow.

She had picked the inn as her base of operations because Victorian Village was not an especially crowded place at this time of year and it was out of the way. Earlier in the day, soon after she'd made a cautious stop at her house in Brimstone to pack a quick suitcase and then take off in her own car, she'd sent a message to Les Beaujack. She'd had it transmitted from the fax machine in a twenty four-hour market in Westport. It said—*I have pictures. You'll have to deal with me now. Will contact you as to terms. (Signed) Buggsy.*

That had amused her at the time, using the dummy's name on the note. Now, though, as she walked toward the small museum, she felt it had been a dumb touch. Juvenile and far from slick.

"This isn't turning out to be much fun," she admitted to herself as she took another look back over her shoulder.

She was absolutely certain that nobody, skimasked or otherwise, had followed her here from the house. But they'd been there again while she was staying with Ben, violated it and torn things apart once more. It was unsettling.

To say the least. Yes, having your home bulldozed by goons can certainly spoil your day.

She didn't especially want to dwell on the sort of people Kathkart and Beaujack had working for them. People who'd tortured poor Rick to make him talk.

"Think about money instead," she urged herself as she pushed open the wooden doors of the museum.

She was the only visitor apparently. The outward room had two reconstructions of nineteenth century interiors, each behind a faded purple plush rope. On the left was a Victorian parlor jammed with clawfooted furniture, flowers, and small statuary under bellglasses and a not very convincing grandfatherly wax dummy slumped in a bentwood rocker and pretending to be reading a tattered copy of *Harper's Weekly*. On the right was a small country kitchen where, with a stuffed cocker spaniel eagerly watching, a plump wax housewife was kneading a loaf of bread.

Same loaf she was working on when Ben and I dropped in.

In the next room, exactly as she'd remembered it, was the display of old carriages—five in all. Still standing at the back was a hearse, five of its six black plumes still extant. Inside the glasswalled vehicle an ornate silver-trimmed black coffin rested on a cradle of planking.

After taking another look behind her, H.J. approached the hearse. She edged along, brushing against the surrey next to it, to the backside of the vehicle and opened the rear door. From her purse she took the envelope of negatives. Reaching into the hearse, and using her other hand to pry one of the lengths of sticky tape loose from her wrist, she slid the envelope beneath the old coffin. She pressed it to the bottom of the black box, smoothed out the strips of tape and withdrew her hand.

A fairly safe hiding place for now.

Carefully shutting the door, she moved away from the old hearse.

Out in the other room now a thin blonde woman and a girl of about six were looking at the nineteenth century kitchen.

"What did they do to that poor doggie?" the perplexed little girl wanted to know.

"Nothing, Vicki, honey."

"Yes, they did, mommy. Did they kill him and stuff him full of cotton?"

"Oh, no, dear, I imagine they simply . . ."

H.J. returned to the sunny afternoon outside.

I ought to feel a hell of a lot happier than I do, she remarked to herself. Within a few days, with any kind of luck, I'll have . . . Well, at least a million dollars. Tax free, since you don't report blackmail earnings on your IRS return.

She walked slowly out of the two-block town and crossed a rustic wooden bridge over a narrow stream to sit on a wrought iron bench beneath a weeping willow.

I really shouldn't have looked up Ben, she decided. He's

like . . . like Jiminy Cricket to me. He can probably even do the voice. Always trying to be my conscience.

Of course, if she hadn't gotten her former husband's help she wouldn't have found out what the hell Rick Dell had been trying to tell her while he was dying. Then she never would have found the film hidden in Buggsy's hollow leg, and she wouldn't be on the brink of wealth.

Or possibly on the brink of the grave.

H.J. crossed her legs, looking out across a wooded hillside.

She'd never done much in the way of landscape painting. Soon, however, with a million dollars or so to play with, she could paint anything she wanted. Or she could paint nothing at all.

No more ripped bodices to paint, no more heaving bosoms, no more dippy beachbum types leering. I'll never have to do a romance cover again.

She leaned back on the bench, trying to look content. But contentment didn't arrive.

"Damn Ben," she said aloud, sitting up straight.

Well, it could be he was right in some ways. Blackmailing the Chumley gang probably wasn't that smart an idea. Maybe, as Ben kept suggesting, she simply ought to turn over all the pictures to the police. Or better yet, mail them in anonymously. Let them go after Kathkart and the rest.

And bid farewell to a million dollars.

The interest on that alone, once you worked a way to deposit it at enough different banks so that the government wouldn't get wise— the interest would be something around $100,000 a year.

Imagine that. More than she'd ever earned in any given year since she'd become a professional artist. Quite a lot more actually, despite the fact she'd hinted to Ben that she was doing nearly as well as he was these days.

I'd better talk to him, she thought, standing up, before I go any further with this.

She'd discuss her feelings with him, not necessarily letting him talk her out of the scheme. But, well, to kick around the pros and cons of dropping the whole damn scheme before somebody came and killed her or arrested her.

Striding rapidly, she headed back toward the inn.

$\triangledown$

20

THE CLOCK IN THE old church tower was striking 3:30 as Ben parked in the treelined lot at the back of Victorian Village Lodge. They were apparently baking apple pies in the nearby kitchen and a pleasant spicy aroma surrounded him as he got out of his car. He was carrying his attache case, to give him an official aura should anyone question his prowling around.

He checked around the parking lot, but didn't spot H.J.'s car. There was no one behind the small horseshoe desk in the quaint hotel lobby. Ben leaned an elbow on the deck, squinted toward the cubbyholes. The one labeled 616 was empty. So H.J. had returned to her room and was pretty likely, even though he hadn't seen her car outside anywhere, to be up there now.

He walked over to the narrow darkwood stairway and started climbing to the third floor. For some reason the 600 rooms were on the third floor of this four story inn. The same flowers-and-vines pattern carpeting was on the quirky flights of stairs as when he and H.J. had stayed here years ago.

"Faith, that was during happier times to be sure," he muttered in his Barry Fitzgerald voice.

H.J.'s room was around a turn in the narrow hallway, just beyond a stunted palm that squatted in a dented, three-legged brass pot. Ben stopped short of the door, when he noticed that it stood about two inches open.

"Not a good sign."

He shoved the door and, ducking low, went on into the room. There was no one inside. But someone had been there, someone besides H.J. The sheets and blankets had been pulled from the bed, the mattress had been removed and dumped on the hardwood floor. All the drawers, from the bureau and the bedside table, lay upended on the hook rug.

Taking a deep breath, Ben quietly shut the door behind him. The closet was empty, no sign of the suitcase he was fairly sure she must've brought here with her. He took a slow walk around the room, looked into the open bathroom. There was nothing in there of interest.

He studied all the floors again more closely, for signs of blood. He found none. Finally he sank into a chintz-covered chair next to the clawfooted phone stand. "Looks like they found her . . . and took her out of here with them."

After a moment, he picked up the phone and pushed the button that gave him an outside line. He phoned his own number to get a playback of his recent messages. It was possible H.J. had gotten away from here on her own and would try to contact him.

"Clutching at straws."

The messages commenced. "This is Chuck Ramsey with Reisberson Brothers Investments, Mr. Spanner. Get back to me about some great buys in—"

"Get off the tape, asshole."

The next voice said, rather plaintively, "This is Candy again, Ben. Are you really ticked off at me or what?"

"Dimwit," he commented.

"Ben, this is Joe. Give me a call. I know who the old gent was."

Then came, "Ben, it's me. Listen, I've been thinking about things and I'd like to talk to you. Call me at—" H.J.'s phone, probably the one he had in his hand now, was abruptly hung up.

"They either walked in on her then," he said. "Or she had second thoughts."

He sat frowning at the phone for nearly a minute. Then he reached into his breast pocket for his address book. He lowered his head, straightened up and punched out a number.

"Lenzer, Moon & Lombard."

"Okay, hon, put me through to Artie Moon," he demanded in his Barry Kathkart voice.

He could hear the young woman on the switchboard inhaling sharply. Very evenly she replied, "As I told you less than twenty minutes go, Mr. Kathkart, Mr. Moon is still away at an important luncheon with a prospective client and simply can't be disturbed for any reason."

"Well, make sure the old fart phones me as soon as he's free. Does he have the number?"

"You're still at home, aren't you?"

"Yeah."

"Then we certainly have the number, Mr. Kathkart."

"Okay, thanks for nothing, bimbo." He hung up, giving a satisfied nod.

He needed a voice to use on Kathkart and now he had one. He needed to know where Kathkart was and now he did. After drumming the fingers of his left hand on the edge of the telephone stand, he phoned the actor's home in Westport. A woman with a sharp nasal voice answered, "Kathkart residence."

"My dear, this is Arthur Moon," Ben said in his Moon voice. "I understand Barry's been trying to get in touch with—"

"You bet your wrinkled up old ass I have, Artie," said Kathkart, coming loudly onto the line. "I think, by the way, you ought to fire that bitch you have answering the—"

"Barry, Barry, calm down, please. Do you have any news about the Mavity girl?"

"I have the Mavity girl, which is what I've been trying to get through to you about."

Ben's grip tightened on the receiver. "She's at your place now, my boy?"

"She will be any minute. Leo and Chico are bringing her here."

"Where was she hiding—"

"I'll give you all the details later, Artie. That little tracking bug they planted in her car paid off," Kathkart said, chuckling. "How soon can you get out here?"

"I'm afraid I won't be able to leave the new client for several more hours, Barry."

"Shit, then we won't be able to question her until I get back from that half-assed personal appearance you and Les talked me into."

"That will be satisfactory, my boy," Ben said, sounding exactly like the advertising executive. "And, please, see to it that she isn't harmed in any way."

"That bitch has given us a lot of trouble. She should be taught— "

"Nevertheless, Barry, I want no further violence."

"Okay, nobody'll hurt her, Artie. Not until we start asking our questions, trust me." Kathkart hung up with a slam of the phone.

Ben next called the Lenzer, Moon & Lombard office once more. "Hi, bimbo. This is your favorite television personality," he told the switchboard, using the Kathkart voice.

"Mr. Kathkart, I've already told you that—"

"Zip your lip, hon, and pay attention. Something has just now come up," he said. "So tell the old fart I won't be home or available on the phone until after my half-assed personal appearance tonight. He can forget bout returning my call until then."

"Very well, Mr. Kathkart. I'll convey that message."

"Love the way you say my name. It'd freeze the balls off a whole tribe of Eskimos. Bye, sweetie."

Hanging up, Ben leaned back again and sighed, then rose and very quietly slipped out of the room.

$\triangledown$

21

"IT'S TOO RISKY."

"I'm going to try anyway."

"Call the police, try your friend Ryerson."

"If I can get her out of Kathkart's on my own the police won't even have to know she was involved in this mess."

"Ben, these guys have kidnapped her. That happens to be a serious crime."

"So is murder Joe. And once H.J. is safe we can tip the police off—anonymously—that Kathkart and his cronies have a couple of murders to their credit."

"Maybe the score will be three before you can do anything about it."

The two men were in Sankowitz's big, whitewalled studio. It was nearly 5:30.

Ben, pacing slowly in front of the row of black filing cabinets, said, "From that fragment of phone message, I'd guess that H.J. was planning to drop the whole damn blackmail idea," he told his friend. "So if I can keep her clear of the law then—"

"For Christ's sake, every cop in this part of the state has a picture of her bending over a corpse," reminded Sankowitz, who was sitting with his back to his drawing board. "So even if you succeeded, possibly with divine intervention, in

114

springing her from those bastards, she'd still—"

"What the police have is a muddy picture of a blurry woman who could be just about anybody."

"Not just anybody, but someone who knew Rick Dell. And by this time they're probably aware that Helen dated the guy."

"So did Trinity Winters, among several others," Ben said. "Now tell me who the victim was."

"What time do you intend to attempt this ill advised Rambo operation?"

"Soon as Kathkart and company leave for his personal appearance. He's due over in Westchester in 8:00, isn't he?"

"According to the newspaper yarn."

"Then he'll be leaving Westport between 6:30 and 7:00. I have to be stationed someplace where I can keep an eye on his mansion not later than 6:15."

"Foolhardy," said the cartoonist. "I'll tell you something. Most of the time you were married to her—at least during the years when I knew the both of you—you were always doing stupid things like this."

"Nope, wrong. I never once rescued H.J. from kidnappers."

"Yeah, but you were forever bailing her out of trouble. If she got a flat tire out in the boondocks, you'd drop everything to rush over there and change it for her rather than letting her phone the damn Triple A. When she was overdrawn on her checking account, you were always the one who—"

"That's love, Joe."

"Bullshit."

"Look, we're chums and all, but I didn't drop by for marriage counseling. Especially since I'm not even married at the moment. Just, c'mon, please, fill me in on what you found out about the old gentleman they carted off in Beaujack's Mercedes."

After a few seconds Sankowitz picked a manilla envelope off the taboret beside his board. He took out two sheets of photocopy paper. "His name was Myron Zepperman, aged seventy-three," he said. "The reason I recognized him is that about five years ago he got a small write up in *People*."

"Who was he?"

"Zepperman, who does look quite a lot like my Uncle Herschel except not so sour, had an unusual occupation. He was chief researcher for *Odd, Isn't it?*."

"That newspaper cartoon panel full of unbelievable facts?"

"Yes, and one of my favorites in my youth. I was especially fond of people who grew potatoes that bore an uncanny resemblance to Richard Nixon. Zepperman, who never got a credit on the panel, supplied most of the oddities for the past forty years."

Ben took the two pages from his friend. They were copies of newspaper obituaries. "Says here he was found dead a couple miles from his home in New Rochelle, New York, eight days ago. The police speculate that he went out for a late night walk and was mugged. His wallet was missing, his watch and so on."

"The alleged mugger beat him so severely that he died of internal injuries. The body was dumped in the alley where it was found."

"That's one of the things we figured they might've done." Ben studied the photo that accompanied the larger obit. "This is sure enough the guy in Rick Dell's pictures."

"Impress on your pea sized brain the part about his being severely beaten," advised Sankowitz. "You could well be the next in line for internal injuries."

"Nope, it was most likely Kathkart who did the beating." He handed the copies back. "Kathkart will be long gone before I hit his place. I wonder why he killed the old man."

"From what you've told me about the Kathkart temperament, it wouldn't take much to incite him to slug somebody."

"Yeah, but what was somebody like Zepperman doing at Kathkart's mansion in the first place?"

"No way of telling for sure," said Sankowitz. "Although one or two possibilities did occur to me."

"Such as?"

"Zepperman was, by profession, somebody who devoted

his days to digging up odd and obscure facts. Possibly, as a sideline, he dug up odd and obscure facts that people paid him to keep quiet about."

"Meaning that Rick Dell was blackmailing them about the murder of a blackmailer?"

"And got murdered for his troubles."

"A mite far fetched maybe, huh? Of course, we have no way of knowing if Zepperman really was a blackmailer."

"No, it isn't something they would have mentioned in that *People* profile."

"Still, it could be an angle that—"

"Why are you two sitting here in the dark?"

"It's not dark, Rhonda my love. Darkness doesn't offic- ially begin in these parts until the sun sets."

A plump blonde woman, decked out in white tennis shorts and a white cardigan, had appeared in the doorway of the studio. "Tell him, Ben, that he'll go blind if he sits around in the dark."

"That is a proven fact, Joe."

"Welcome home, darling," Sankowitz said in the direc- tion of his wife. "Go away."

She reached over and clicked on the light switch. "How are you, Ben? You don't look especially worried for someone who's facing a long term in prison."

"Prison?" He looked from her to her husband.

"From what Joe's been telling me about your escapades over the past few days, I'd guess five to ten in the slammer," said Rhonda amiably. "Would you like some organic grapes and a cup of herbal tea?"

"Maybe I ought to have bread and water instead, to get in training for prison life."

She said, "As I recall, H.J. was perpetually leading you astray during your turbulent marriage."

"So all the gossip columns proclaimed."

Sankowitz told her, "Loved one, this isn't England and nobody wishes afternoon tea. Scram."

"Ben looks as though he hasn't eaten for a week."

"Actually he looks like an overstuffed sofa," countered her

husband. "Begone, dear, and allow us to finish our important and private conversation."

Rhonda said, "I think it's very Christian of you to have anything at all to do with H.J., considering all the grief she caused you."

"Well, it's a well known fact that I'm in line for sainthood."

"Rhonda, really now, take your leave."

"He never likes me to drop in on him in his studio here," she told Ben. "Most normal people, thank you very much, find me most comforting. Over at the Brimstone Hospice, where I do volunteer work twice each week, they think of my visits as—"

"We're not dying is the trouble," her husband pointed out. "Were we bound for immediate glory, I'm sure we'd both delight in having you hang around."

"I guess I'll change and shower. Would you like a plate of oat bran and carob chip cookies, Ben?"

"Not really, no."

"Well, good luck with the tremendous botch you've made of your life." Smiling, she took her leave.

"Do you have a gun I can borrow?" Ben asked the cartoonist.

"You'd need silver bullets for Rhonda."

"No, I mean a gun I can take along with me to—"

"This isn't the local chapter of the NRA."

"What's that over there on the bookcase?"

Sankowitz turned to look in the direction he was pointing. "Merely a prop, a Colt Six Shooter. Barrel's plugged."

"Can I borrow it?"

"I guess so, sure. But I think guys who stick knives in comics and beat up gents in their seventies aren't going to be much intimidated by a prop cowboy gun."

Ben went over, picked up the gun, thrust it in his waistband and pulled his sport coat over to conceal the protruding butt of the weapon. "Might come in handy."

"Be careful when you sit down now. It's quite easy to drive the barrel right down into your groin."

"*Helpful Hints On Gunhandling* by Joseph Sankowitz." He checked his wristwatch. "I'd better be going."

"What time do you intend to burst in?"

"At the latest it'll be a little after 7."

"Forget it," advised Sankowitz. "Stay right here and call the law."

"No, I have to give it a try."

"Maybe you ought to stop long enough for those cookies and some tea. Could be your last meal."

"I'll see you." Ben, adjusting the sixshooter, headed for the doorway.

$\triangledown$

22

A VERY UNINTERESTING SHADE of brown, roughly the color of peanut butter after it's been exposed to the air for several days. She awoke to find herself surrounded by it.

H.J. contemplated her possible location for a moment and then decided she might get more information if she opened her eyes further.

That proved to be an extremely unpleasant experience. Too much light came rushing in and a very jittery display of dancing specks started up. Even shutting her eyes didn't stop the light show. It reminded her of something second rate Canadian animators might have turned out.

She tried opening her eyes again, though more slowly and carefully this time. The godawful shade of brown was emanating from the rough woolen blanket she found she was sprawled on face down. The blanket, she determined by prodding it with the hand she wasn't lying on top of, seemed to be part of a bed.

But sure as hell not the bed in . . . In where?

H.J. had the feeling she'd been until recently somewhere other than here. Wherever here might be.

Victoria Station?

Not quite right.

Victorian Village?

That sounded like it. Yes, she'd been in her room at the inn there. Doing what?

Talking on the phone, she answered silently.

Right, she'd been talking to her husband. Well, not her husband anymore, but she knew whom she meant. She'd telephoned Ben. But she hadn't talked to him, only to his answering machine.

She made a faint, rusty, moaning sound. Her right arm, just below the shoulder, hurt a lot. Somebody had stuck a needle in her. H.J. remembered that now.

I hope it was a clean needle.

Be a shame to get AIDS or hepatitis or lockjaw not what she'd decided to become a better person.

How was she going to do that exactly?

It had something to do with Ben. Oh, sure, right. By telling him she needed his help again. Only this time she wanted him to help her get rid of all of Rick's damn pictures.

The pictures. Where the hell were they?

Easy now, don't panic.

She'd hidden the negatives in a safe place. In the coffin with the ventriloquist and his dummy at . . . No, not there. A coffin, though. That was it, under the coffin at the Village museum. The contact prints, though, were in her purse. And she had no idea where her purse had gotten to.

She'd been phoning Ben and then the door of the bathroom had come swinging open. A man came out, a big man in a dark windbreaker and dark slacks, wearing a skimask. Before she could say anything about him into the phone, a second man—he must have been in the closet— had grabbed her from behind. He slapped a hand over her mouth, twisted the phone out of her hand and hung it up. Then he—or maybe it was the other one—had stuck a hypodermic in her arm and shot something harsh and burning into her.

That had happened . . . well, she had no idea now long ago that had been. She'd passed out as soon as they stuck the damn needle into her. Well, no. First she'd felt suddenly very sick to her stomach and then she'd become dizzy. After that she passed out.

Now she took a few careful breaths in and out. Her lungs still seemed to be working. Now to find out how some of the other important parts were functioning. Legs, arms, and so on.

That was, you know, really stupid. Letting them jump you so easily.

H.J. had no idea how they'd been able to find her at the inn. She was absolutely certain no one had tailed her from Westport over into Westchester County.

Okay, she'd figure it out later. Right now she needed to put all her effort into getting up off that bed.

She twisted, managing to pull the hand she was lying on out from under her pelvis. It was numb and her fingers started hurting when she tried wiggling them back to life. Finally, after a few rough minutes, she managed to do a shaky pushup. Then, struggling, she was able to swing her legs around. The light show played a return engagement.

When her vision cleared, she noticed she was sitting on the edge of a narrow cot that was pushed back against the wall in a small, windowless room with pale tan walls. She also saw that there was a large, wide man in dark clothing seated in a wicker chair less than five feet from her. He was no longer wearing his skimask and a faint grin showed on his rough, weatherbeaten face.

H.J. eyed him. "I thought," she said in a creaky voice, "I was alone."

"I been guarding you," he explained. "That hasn't been too bad, especially since you got such a cute little ass."

Ben jerked upright, tossed the binoculars on the passenger seat and turned around to see who had started pounding on his car window.

There was a husky, tweedy man with a bristling white moustache hitting on the glass with a gloved left hand.

Rolling down the window less than four inches, he inquired, "Yeah?"

"What the hell do you think you're doing?"

Ben had parked his car off the road on the street above the one where Kathkart's white mansion sat. From up here, using the binoculars he'd just bought at a sporting goods shop, he could get a fine view of the driveways.

He tried his tough Robert DeNiro voice. "What do you think I'm doing here?"

"This is a private road and you've probably come here to drink beer," said the annoyed man. "They do it most every night, although unusually much later than this. Park here, drip crankcase oil on the greenery, guzzle beer, toss beer cans, cigarettes and God knows what all around."

The dog tried to get one of his paws into the car far enough to touch Ben. He whimpered when he failed.

"I wasn't aware I was trespassing," said Ben, still tough but a bit conciliatory. He was parked on a stretch of weedy grass. There was a low stone fence and a field beyond that, but no sign of a house nearby.

"It's not my property, but I live just over the hill." The man gestured with his heavy, gnarled walking stick. "I've lived there for almost nine years, a long time by Westport standards. Most of them around here, they come and they go. All at the whim of some giant corporation or other."

"Yeah, that's sure true. In fact, that's why I happen to be here."

"What's why?"

"I'm doing some checking on a top corporate executive."

"Which executive might that be? As I understand things, that fool television fishmonger lives down below."

"He does, true. But this exec's wife is suspected of . . . Well, I need say no more."

The white-moustached man tapped his stick thoughtfully on the ground a few times. "I suppose you do have your job to do."

"Don't we all. You're very understanding."

"You won't be drinking any beer?"

"Not while on duty, it's against the rules."

"There isn't likely to be any shooting, is there?"

Ben shifted on his seat, causing the sixshooter to dig into his thigh. "Oh, no. Hell, this is nothing more than a very routine surveillance job."

The man brought his stick up and stroked his prominent chin with it. "Very well, I'll continue with my walk and leave you to your work," he said. "I assume you also won't be playing loud rock and roll on your car radio?"

"That would spoil the element of surprise."

Nodding, he said, "Good evening then. Come along, Togo."

The dog gave a final whimper before dropping away.

Ben waited impatiently until they'd walked several hundred feet uphill, then grabbed the binoculars again.

$\triangledown$

23

He WAS MY MAN Chumley when he came into the little room. Full butler rig, including black tail coat, silvery hair slicked down.

"You damn bitch," began Kathkart.

"There was no need," she said from the corner where she was standing, "to dress so formally."

"I don't have all that much time right now," the actor told her. "But when I get back from this stupid personal appearance, we'll have a nice long conversation. As long as it takes, Miss Mavity."

"That'll give me something to look forward to."

"How'd your shirt get torn?"

"It's the trend around here."

Frowning at the big man over near the door, Kathkart asked him, "What did I tell you, Chico?"

"Watch the broad till she woke up. Then get hold of you."

"Asshole—what else?"

Chico didn't meet the other's eyes. "Don't mess with her."

"What was that you just mumbled? I didn't quite catch it."

"You told me not to fool around with her, Barry. And I didn't— hardly at all."

"While we're gone," Kathkart told him, "I want you to stay out in the hall. You comprehend?"

"Yeah, sure. But it's not like I molested her or anything serious. Only just, you know, a little fooling around—"

"Get the hell out of here. Now!"

"She's only some dumb bitch, so I don't see why—"

"Out. Get out."

Giving an annoyed grunt, the big man left them.

Kathkart grinned at H.J. "You know, hon, it occurs to me that if you don't tell me exactly what I want to know, I just might let that ape loose on you afterall."

"You look like the kind of man that sort of idea would occur to."

"The photos," he said, "the ones we found in your purse. Is that the entire set, is that all of them?"

She nodded slowly. "Yes."

"Fine, hon." The actor moved closer to her. "Now here's the important question. Where are the negatives?"

She blinked. "What are you trying to do?"

"The negatives, sweetheart, where did you stash them?"

"If you have the pictures, you must have the negatives, too," she insisted. "Everything, the whole works, was in my purse. Could be Chico and his buddy are holding out on you."

He glanced over at the door. Then, chuckling, he shook his head. "Nice try, but no cheroot," Kathkart said. "Chico and Leo are too dumb *and* too chickenshit to try anything like that."

"Are they?"

"I want the negatives." He walked up to her. "I'll get them out of you, too. Tonight, tomorrow at the very latest, you'll tell me where they are."

"I'm telling you right now. They were in my purse along with the prints."

"If that were true, I wouldn't need you at all," said Kathkart, laughing. "No, not at all. See, I'd get Leo and Chico to give me the negatives, then I'd tell them to get rid of you."

"I see."

"So maybe you better forget your bluff and tell me the truth."

"And then what happens? Don't I still get handed over to your goons?"

"We can work something out."

"Such as?"

"Listen, I'm getting tired of all this chitchat," he warned. "You tell me and then we'll make a deal."

"I don't see how that would be to my advant—"

"Tell me!" He swung out with his right hand, slapping her, hard, across the face.

She pressed back against the wall. "Careful, you don't want to get blood on your nice uniform." She touched at her cheek.

"I'm not in the mood for any more—"

"This isn't at all wise, old buddy." Les Beaujack had quietly entered the room.

"Don't you start—"

"I'm serious, Barry. Leave her alone." He nodded at H.J. "I apologize for this, Miss Mavity."

"Oh, sure. Up to now it's been simply a nice, pleasant kidnapping," she said. "Then he had to go spoil it with rough stuff."

"I don't especially," said Kathkart, "like your kind of smartass—"

"Back off, Barry."

Kathkart frowned at him. "Don't start talking to me like I'm one of those dogs you and your wife raise."

He took the actor by the arm. "We're late as it is, so let's get going."

Kathkart produced a few grumbling noises deep in his chest. "If you hadn't set up this half-assed appearance, I—"

"The simplest thing to do, old buddy, is just to go and do it."

"Okay, okay." He spun around, brushed by the advertising executive and went stomping into the hall.

Beaujack smiled cautiously at H.J. "I'm sorry this happened. However, if—"

"I know. If I don't cooperate, you'll turn him loose on me."

"That exactly, I'm afraid, what will happen." His smile slowly faded away. "Think about it while we're gone."

At three minutes before seven Ben said, "Finally." The day had begun to fade about a half hour before and the lights had blossomed inside the house a few minutes later.

Now a grey Mercedes came rushing onto the circular front driveway of Kathkart's estate. It jerked to a stop a few feet short of the front door. Les Beaujack hurried out and up onto the porch. The big white door opened halfway, framing Beaujack briefly in a rectangle of yellow before he stepped inside.

I don't think they have hurt her yet, Ben told himself. But that was more a hope than a conviction. H.J. might well be dead already. Maybe Joe was right. This was something for the police.

"Too late for that now."

What the hell was Beaujack doing in there? All he had to do was pick up Kathkart and take him over to Westchester.

Twilight was closing in now. It would be difficult pretty soon to see what was going on.

At nine minutes after seven the front door opened. Beaujack was the first out, followed by Kathkart in his full Chumley rig. The two of them seemed to be arguing, and as Beaujack started to get into the backseat, the burly actor caught his shoulder and yanked him around. Hands on hips, Kathkart continued facing him and shouting about something. None of their words got as far as Ben.

Trinity Winters emerged from the house next. She was wearing white jeans and a hip-length mink.

Behind her came a large, broadshouldered man in dark clothes. He shut the door to the house and, tossing what might be a set of keys in his right hand, got in behind the wheel.

"That must be either Leo or Chico," Ben muttered, narrowing his eyes and straining to see down through the gathering dusk. Kathkart had mentioned the two names on the phone and it was safe to assume both were hired muscle. "So if that's Chico, Leo could still be at home and keeping watch on H.J."

Shaking her head, Trinity started tugging at Kathkart's sleeve. He turned angrily, and yelled at her but climbed into the back seat. Trinity said something to Beaujack before joining Kathkart. The adman shrugged and took a seat in front next to the driver.

A moment later the car's lights snapped on and it went roaring around the driveway onto the street.

Ben, fingers drumming on the steering wheel, waited a long five minutes. "No sign of Arthur Moon, so this ought to work," he said as he started the engine.

He drove quietly away from his observation post.

24

THE GAS STATION HE'D picked out earlier was on the Post Road, a little over a mile from Kathkart's. Ben swung his car off the street, parking a few feet from the phone stand. He slid out of his car and trotted over to it. Not until he was reaching for the instrument did he see the small sign, printed in pencil on an orange sheet of memo paper and taped to the phone—*Out of order.*

"Shit," remarked Ben, looking around.

There was a Chinese restaurant in the small shopping plaza next to the station. They'd have a phone.

He hit the sidewalk, jogged along and pushed through the scarlet and gold door of Lee's Gardens.

A slim waiter smiled at him in the foyer. "Table for one, sir?"

"Do you have a telephone?"

The man shook his head apologetically. "Have a telephone, but is out of order."

Ben returned to the street. This was futzing things up. He had to make a call before he could proceed with the rest of his plan for rescuing H.J.

"Ah, across the street." There was a kiosk on the other side of the wide twilit street, at the edge of the parking lot that bordered a shut-down discount appliance store.

Dodging the heavy traffic, ignoring the honking and the shouts, he ran over to it.

There was now a fat young man using the phone. He had somehow materialized there while Ben had been concentrating on avoiding the cars on the Post Road.

". . . be that way, is there, Jen?" the young man was saying pleadingly into the mouthpiece. "I'd only stay honestly, about a half hour or so tonight. What? I didn't intend to be disrespectful the other night, Jen, not at all. Yes, I did do that, but . . . You want something, mister?"

"I'm Dr. Mackinson," explained Ben in his E.G. Marshall voice. "It's vitally important, young man, that I have access to this phone."

"Don't you have a phone in your car? I thought all medical men . . . Hang on a second, Jen. No, honestly, I'm not ignoring you. Really I am sorry I tried to grab you the other night and I won't do that tonight if you'll only let me drop over . . . Doc, maybe you ought to find another telephone, huh? I may be here for—"

"This happens to be the only working phone in the area. And a little girl's life hangs in the balance."

That fat young man tugged at the front of his sweatshirt and turned his back to the phone. "Really? What sort of case is it?"

"You probably heard about the accident on the Metro North track this afternoon. The poor child's toes were—"

"No, I didn't. See, I've been arguing with my girlfriend from various telephones for most of the day and I missed the television news."

"I must contact the hospital—"

"Jen, hold on awhile longer, will you," he said into the phone. "No, I really do love you and I don't have another woman with me. You're not being logical, since I'm standing out here in the middle of the Post Road. And, hey, I didn't take off all my clothes in your living room the other night. Jen, a T-shirt isn't, by any stretch of the imagination, all of a person's wardrobe. What do you mean by that? I happen to dress very—"

"The phone," interrupted Ben. "I really must—"

"I'm winning her over, doctor. If I can just talk to her for a few more—"

"I happen to be a specialist in feminine psychology and—"

"I thought your specialty was sewing toes back on little girls?"

"That, too. The point is, young man, that you aren't approaching your problem in the proper manner at all," said Ben, struggling to control his impatience. "What you must do is quit pleading and go over to her house and walk right in." He yanked out his wallet, grabbed out a ten dollar bill. "Get a pizza and a six pack to take along."

"You think that would work on Jen?"

"It always works. It's basic feminine psychology."

The young man snapped the bill from between Ben's fingers. "Jen, I have to go. There's an emergency here. I can't explain now." He hung up the phone. "Good luck, doctor, and thanks."

As soon as the youth was trotting toward his car, Ben dropped a coin in the phone and punched out a number.

"Kathkart residence." It was the same nasal voiced woman. One more person, in addition to either Leo or Chico, who was still at home.

"This is Arthur Moon, my dear," he said in his Moon voice. "Let me speak to Barry if you would."

"I'm afraid, Mr. Moon, that you just missed him."

"I suspected I might," he said. "Very well, this then is what we'll have to do. Barry happens to be in possession of some recent Chumley statistics that I must make use of this evening and as soon as possible.

"I wasn't aware that any new—"

"Well, my dear you know how he can be, very cavalier at times. At any rate, I really need the material ASAP," he continued. "What I'd—"

"If I can find it, I can fax it right to you."

"Alas I'm not near any of my fax machines just now," he said. "Would it be all right if I sent a young man over there immediately to pick the material up?"

"I suppose so, Mr. Moon, except that I don't know exactly where it is."

"This young fellow will be able to identify the report in question. If you'll admit him to Barry's sanctum, I'm reasonably confident he'll find it without any trouble."

"Well, yes, then. That would, I guess, be okay," she said. "What's his name."

"His name," Ben answered, "is Jennings Lee. A very likeable and efficient junior account executive at LM&L. Thank you very much for your help in this crisis, my dear."

As he did some broken field running back through the traffic, he allowed himself a gratified smile. So far everything was going fairly smoothly.

He drove right back onto the estate grounds this time. Darkness had taken over, filling in everything all around the house.

"Good evening, I'm Jennings Lee," he was saying aloud as he guided his car around the wide, whitegraveled drive. He was trying out his William F. Buckley voice, but that didn't sound quite right for the part.

No, what was called for was something more upbeat and likeable.

"Hi, I'm Jennings Lee," he said in a Tom Hanks sort of voice.

Much better. You'd trust a guy with a voice like that.

"Greetings, gate, let's percolate. I'm Jennings Lee," he said in his Jerry Colonna voice. Very few people would recognize the voice of Bob Hope's one time sidekick. Unless like Ben they liked to listen to tapes of old radio shows to pick up new ideas for voices. But this last was entirely for his own benefit, because he was feeling increasingly uneasy.

Parking in front of the row of garages, he turned off the lights and the engine. From the backseat he fetched his attache case. It made a good prop in this situation, too. A cleancut, sincere adman always carried at least one.

"Good evening, ma'am. I'm Jennings Lee. Mr. Moon . . .

um . . . telephoned you about me." Tom Hanks again and it sounded exactly right.

He left the car and started swinging the case at his side in a lively, innocent Madison Avenue manner.

He went hurrying up the three brick steps, pushed the doorbell and straightened the tie he'd chosen earlier.

The door opened wide. Arthur Moon was smiling out at him, a .32 revolver in his hand. "Timing, as a gifted actor such as yourself well knows, Mr. Spanner, is everything," he said pleasantly. "I arrived five minutes after your very inventive call to Miss Spaulding. Had I not arrived until a half hour from now, whatever you have in mind would have had a much better chance of working. Please come in, won't you?"

$$\triangledown$$

25

"I T WASN'T THAT SERIOUS, really, Ben."

"The guy attempts to rape you and—"

"I doubt Chico's capable of that."

"That's Chico? The one out in the hall with the .45 automatic resting in his lap."

"We weren't formally introduced, but that's what Kathkart called him." She was sitting on the narrow cot, watching Ben pace the blank room.

"Okay, so in the house at the moment we have—far as I know—Moon, Chico and Miss Spaulding."

"Who's she?"

"I'd have guessed private secretary, except she's currently roaming around upstairs carrying what looks to be a sawed-off shotgun."

"Then the whole household is in cahoots," observed H.J. "Guess that figures, since everybody will lose a cut of the pie if Kathkart ends up in the pokey."

Slightly hunched, Ben was staring up at the low ceiling. "I haven't been able to spot any listening bugs, but we'd better go on the assumption that we aren't having a private conversation down here."

"How far down are we, by the way—in the basement?"

"Yep, Moon escorted me down from the ground floor. This

room is part of a cluster of three or four alongside the furnace room."

"You think Kathkart instructed his architect to add a few little out of the way rooms where he could stick prisoners and torture people now and then?"

"With enough money you can order anything," he said. "You sure you're okay?"

"How so—physically or spiritually?"

"I don't like the idea that they drugged you."

"All things considered, that was probably better than a clout on the skull with a lead pipe." She rested her elbows on her knees. "What I can't understand, Ben, is how they knew I was at the inn at all."

"They planted some kind of tracking gimmick in your car."

"Then I shouldn't have gone back to my place to pick it up. When I didn't see anybody lurking around, though, I assumed—"

"Why'd you try to phone me?"

"Oh, you got the message? I wish I'd had the opportunity to scream or pass on some clever coded message."

"I found you anyway, though this may not end up being a rescue mission."

"How *did* you locate me?"

After completing a slow circuit of the room, Ben seated himself on the cot close beside her and put an arm around her shoulders. "Up until I got here I'd been feeling fairly smart and smug," he began, and then gave her a concise, edited account of what he'd been up to since he'd awakened in the morning to find her gone.

H.J. leaned over and kissed him. "Very commendable."

He asked, "So what was the call about?"

"Well, bright and early I sent a teasing fax to Beaujack, hinting that I had Rick's stuff and to stand by for my price list," his former wife told him. "But by early afternoon I'd pretty much concluded I wasn't cut out to be a blackmailer. It may also be that I had a premonition those two louts were about to catch up with me. Anyway, I was going to ask you to come and get me."

"Timing," murmured Ben.

"What?"

"Our timing seems to have been off at several crucial points today."

H.J. sighed. "I'm afraid you've had a rather negative effect on my criminal instincts. There I was, enjoying the idea that very soon I'd have so much money I'd never have to paint another godawful romance cover. Then my conscience—and since I didn't have one earlier, it must be something I caught from you—went to work on me. I knew it was time to call the whole thing off."

"That proves you're capable of being salvaged."

"I'm really worried that neither one of us is going to be salvaged this time," she said, taking hold of his hand. "We'll probably end up being recycled into plant food."

"Maybe not."

"C'mon, be realistic. We know that several very rich people, all of whom wish to continue to be rich, are involved in murder," she reminded him. "They killed poor Rick and that other gentleman and they're likely to kill us because we know about it."

"The old gent's name was Zepperman."

"How'd you find that out?"

"Research. It may turn out that he was a blackmailer, too."

"That would be ironic, huh? Kathkart kills a blackmailer and then finds out he's being blackmailed about that."

Ben said softly, "Without giving any specifics, H.J., tell me about the photos."

She replied, "They've got the prints now, since I was carrying them in my purse."

"What about the negatives?"

"Hidden," she whispered.

Nodding, he said, "Then maybe we can still get out of this."

"You think so?"

"Yeah." He leaned closer, kissing her on the cheek. Next to her ear he said, "If I can get one of them in here alone, faint when I do my Ronald Colman voice."

"Who is—"

There was a knock on the door.

Moon came into their cell, alone. Shutting the door, he leaned against it. He was holding his revolver in his right hand, with his left cupped under the handle. "I thought," he told them, "we might have a sensible talk before the others return."

Ben stood up. "Somebody around here had better turn sensible," he said. "You folks might be able to get away with one or two murders, but three or four is going to be much trickier."

"Perhaps we can avoid any further killing," said the agency head.

"Your stooges haven't been especially bright," Ben said. "It should have been obvious, after H.J. sent her first message to Beaujack, that we're not in this to expose anybody."

"You and the young lady are partners, is that it?"

"What else would we be?" said H.J., picking up on Ben's bluffing.

"She's been wavering on this," said Ben, "but now that I'm here we are definitely going ahead with it."

"Interesting how you can work together even after a divorce."

"For fifty percent of a million dollars," said Ben, "I'd work with a lot worse people than her."

"Same here." Smiling sweetly, she rose slowly from the cot.

"That's your price, is it, one million?"

Ben answered, "Actually it's the down payment."

"A million now," explained H.J., wandering over to the opposite side of the room from Ben, "and another million when we turn the pictures over to you."

"As I understand it, my dear, we already have the photos. The negatives are what we—"

"You have *one* set of prints," corrected Ben. "There are two others. One safely hidden and one with an attorney in a sealed envelope. That'll go directly to a friend of mine who's a cop if H.J. and I stay missing too long."

"Then there are the negatives," said H.J. "Those are also hidden away, but not in the same place as the prints. Considering all you're getting, Mr. Moon, $2,000,000 is a bargain price.'

"There's one other thing that's essential," he said, glancing from one to the other. "That, of course, is your silence."

"We'll throw that in for nothing," Ben assured him, taking two steps in his direction. "As soon as we have the money, we guarantee we won't talk."

"There's a much cheaper way," said Moon, smiling. "A more economical method of assuring that you remain silent."

"The more people you kill, the greater the chances of your being caught," H.J. pointed out. "Keep in mind, too, that if we don't contact our lawyer by tomorrow—early—he's going to rush a full set of pictures to the police. Nice shots of you and your cronies getting rid of Mr. Zepperman."

"You know his name, I see."

"Sure, we know just about everything."

Ben added, "All of which we'll forget—for a fee."

"We're being very reasonable, too," said H.J., "considering the enormous amount of money you people pull in off the Chumley account."

"Yes, yes. That was the argument Barry Kathkart used when he persuaded us to help him cover up his impetuous crime."

"Why don't you let us go now?" suggested Ben, edging another step closer.

"As much as I dislike Leo and Chico, I have to admit they're efficient," said Moon. "Without any doubt they can make you talk. It might take time and be unpleasant, but it would save us $2,000,000, wouldn't it?"

"You aren't the sort," said H.J., "who'd condone torture."

"That's a flattering appraisal of my character, my dear. Until quite recently it might have been true, but in the past few days I've crossed several lines I never believed I'd cross."

"If you aren't going to turn us loose, maybe I'd better start rehearsing some farewell speeches," said Ben, taking another step. "You know, like 'It's a far, far better thing I do than I have ever done before.'" He waited a few seconds and then eyed his former wife.

She didn't immediately respond. "Oh, was that your Robert Colman voice?"

"Ronald Colman."

"I don't know why I didn't recognize it, darling, since it's always been one of . . ." She began to sway slightly. "That's funny, I'm feeling . . . What was I saying? Oh, yes. Don't you think it's absolutely wonderful how Ben can do so many . .

Jesus, it feels like one of my spells, Ben . . . I . . ." She bent, clutching at her midsection. Then her eyes went wide and started to roll. She straightened up, arms going straight out at her sides. She fell to her knees, flapped her arms, moaned, fell over on her side with her feet kicking convulsively.

Moon was distracted, lowering his gun and staring at the fallen and apparently seriously stricken young woman.

Ben took advantage of his inattention and jumped. He chopped at the older's man thin right wrist. Moon let go of the gun and Ben caught it before it hit the floor. Swinging up with the gun barrel, he caught Moon in the chin. Then as he fell, Ben used the butt of the revolver against his temple, twice.

He slid his arm around the torso of the unconscious adman, dragged him over to the cot and let him fall atop it.

Outside the door Chico called out, "You okay in there, Mr. Moon?"

"Yes, yes," answered Ben in his Moon voice as, gun in hand, he moved over to station himself beside the door. "But I'm afraid something terrible has happened to the young lady. Come in here, Chico, quickly."

26

"THAT WAS A VERY impressive swoon, by the way."

"You think perhaps I overdid it a bit?"

"Flapping your arms was maybe too much frosting, yeah."

"It sure worked, though, huh?"

"We distracted Moon good and proper."

The advertising executive was now stretched out on the cot, his arms tied behind him with his belt and his ankles bound with his paisley tie. For a gag they'd use his crisp display handkerchief.

Chico was face down on the floor, snarling. He was hogtied with strips of the brown blanket, since he wore neither a belt nor a tie.

While Ben stood over him with the .32 revolver in one hand and Chico's .45 automatic in the other, H.J. finished attaching a gag made of another strip of blanket.

Smiling, she knelt and patted the thug once on the backside. "That's a mighty cute little ass you've got there yourself," she said, standing up.

"What's that for?" asked Ben. "Part of some old Girl Scout ritual?"

"A personal touch," she answered. "I'll explain sometime."

Easing over to the door, Ben opened it a few inches.

"Apparently they can't hear what's going on down here from upstairs." He looked cautiously out into the hall.

"We really don't know how many of them there are left up there."

"Beyond the secretary, no."

"Possibly there could be more goons."

He handed her the revolver. "Possibly." He stepped out of their cell. The only sound down here was the rattling and humming of the big furnace.

"We make a pretty good team," she said quietly, taking hold of his hand.

"At times." They started along the dimly it corridor. "On the way down I didn't notice any doors leading directly out of this basement. So we're going to have to go back up into the house and exit from there."

"It's interesting how money affects some people."

"With you as a prime example?"

"No, I was thinking of Arthur Moon. He is a respected advertising executive *and* a snappy dresser—but I got the feeling he was going to go ahead and let them torture us and then terminate us as well."

"I got that impression, too. Which is why I did my Ronald Colman signal to you."

"*Ronald* Colman. He was some kind of movie actor, right?"

"Skip it—and let's be quiet for the rest of our journey."

"It's cute the way you get ticked off over something trivial while we're in the midst of a struggle for our very—"

"Quiet," he snapped.

The first shotgun blast missed them by a little less than six feet. Pellets spattered across a stretch of peach colored wall in the large oval foyer, chewing away sizeable bites of plaster and molding.

Ben had tumbled H.J. to the floor with him, getting off a shot at the chunky blonde secretary, who was standing on the staircase across the way.

His shot was wild, too, and it went smashing up into one

of the dangling crystal chandeliers, producing a raucous wind-chimes sort of noise.

Rolling across the slick hardwood floor, Ben dragged his erstwhile wife through the first open doorway they came to. "That was the lady I was telling you about."

"The secretary with the shotgun."

"Her, yes." He got to his feet in what looked to be some sort of trophy room.

"She's not a crack shot." H.J. scrambled upright, slamming the door behind her.

"She may just be warming up." He pushed her clear of the doorway.

They were surrounded by My Man Chumley items, including a lifesize cardboard cutout of Kathkart in the role, dozens of framed posters and magazine ads, and even a large fat Chumley beanbag that looked a good deal like the actor.

After getting H.J. to a safe spot, Ben shoved a black leather sofa in front of the door.

H.J. said, "French doors over yonder."

"We'll try them as a way out." He gathered her up and they hurried to the glass doors.

A tremendous wham sounded behind them and a sizeable portion of the door they'd just shut came exploding into the room in the form of splintery chunks of white-painted wood. The jagged scraps and the shotgun pellets ripped the head clean off the stand-up cardboard Chumley.

"Let's get going." Ben pushed one of the French doors open. He stepped out onto the flagstone terrace, scanned the immediate area and then helped H.J. out into the night with him.

"What next?" she asked.

"My car's out in front of the garages—at least that's where I left it. But they may've moved it or futzed with it."

"That leaves escape on foot."

"Across the back lawn here and up into the woods." He took hold of her arm and they started running across the acre of grass at the rear of the mansion. Less than thirty seconds later lights came to life on all sides of them. The estate had floodlights planted all around its borders.

They kept running and were soon high enough to see down across the top of the house and get a glimpse of the front drive. The Mercedes had just turned onto the grounds.

"They're back." Ben was commencing to wheeze some.

"We can outrun them."

"Miss Spaulding's out there, pointing up at us."

"Shit, they're going to drive the damn car up here after us."

The Mercedes, the beams of its headlights bouncing and making wild zigzags across the blackness, left the drive and was roaring up across the green.

Ben took a quick, appraising look around. "They'll cut us off before we can climb all the way into the woods," he said. "Let's head for that big shed over there."

As they changed their course, she asked, "Can we hold them off?"

"For awhile maybe, and once we start shooting it should attract attention." He slipped an arm around her waist and accelerated the pace. "Hopefully the shotgun blasts have already attracted attention."

They made it through the front door of the long low wooden shed just as the Mercedes came around the side of the big white mansion.

After slamming the door shut, Ben stationed himself at the small dusty window that faced the approaching car. "Holy Christ."

"What?"

"I don't think they're going to stop. Looks like they're going to slam into the shed."

H.J. went stumbling through the place, trying to avoid colliding with the scatter of sacks of peat moss and the assorted mowers, leafblowers, wheelbarrows, and rakes. "There's another door in back," she said, catching his hand and pulling him after her.

"That's got to be Kathkart at the wheel. He's the only one goofy enough to think he's driving a tank."

The nose of the Mercedes came ripping into the front door. The door and the entire front wall broke in huge pieces and the pieces came spinning back into the tangle of equipment. Metal buckled and shrieked, sacks exploded, rakes and hoes pinwheeled up into the air. Glass broke and one of the car's front tires popped with a stuttering blast.

Ben and H.J. dived out the back way and went rolling and tumbling across the wet grass.

"You all right?" he asked.

She didn't answer. She was lying on the lawn, sprawled, the revolver fallen from her hand and lying several feet from her slack fingers.

"H.J." He knelt close to her, noticing now the bloody streak across her forehead and the deep gash in her cheek.

He took her hand, rubbing at it. He had no idea why he was doing that.

She moaned faintly.

Then from downhill came the hooting of a siren. A patrol car had turned into the Kathkart driveway. Close behind it came a civilian car.

"That's Detective Ryerson bringing up the rear I think," murmured Ben. "H.J., you've got to wake up."

"Oh boy," she said faintly, sucking in a breath of air.

"Anything broken?"

"Don't think so. Something whacked me on the side of the head as we were taking our leave of the shed. Knocked me out for a minute I guess."

Very gently, he helped her into a sitting position. "The police seem to have arrived. Those shotgun blasts must've annoyed the neighbors sufficiently to—"

"You shits! You god damn assholes." Kathkart, his Chumley costume in disarray, staggered into view from around the shattered shed with a .38 revolver waving in his fist. "Look at all the frigging trouble you've caused me."

"Toss away the gun." Ben had his borrowed .45 pointed straight at the charging actor.

"Like hell, like bloody hell, Spanner," he said advancing. "Everything was going fine . . . that blackmailing bastard Zepperman had been taken care of and everybody was believing the old fart had been mugged and not strangled by me . . . then her snooping boyfriend pops up . . . and then we get rid of him okay . . . and she . . . she gets her hands on the pictures and it starts all over again . . . she tries to blackmail me . . . I'm going to fix both of you so—"

"Mr. Kathkart, sir." The tall, blond Detective Ryerson was climbing up across the brightly lit lawn. He had a .38 revolver in his hand. "If you'd drop that gun now—drop yours, too, Ben—then we can have a nice, calm talk and get everything sorted out."

Kathkart didn't comply. Instead he gave an angry growl and spun around to face the policeman.

"Put the gun down, sir."

Kathkart fired it instead.

Dodging, Ryerson fired back.

Kathkart missed, but the detective's slug took the actor square in the chest.

He roared once, both his arms went out wide. He let go his gun and it went bouncing away. He danced backward across the grass, flatfooted, for a half dozen steps. The tails of his black coat flapped and swirled. Then he stopped suddenly still, started teetering, lurched to his right. he dropped to the ground, toppled over on his face and was dead.

H.J. squeezed Ben's arm. "Even the butler was poor," she said.

It was exactly midnight when they came into Fagin's diner. The proprietor was sitting at his own counter, smoking a cigarette and reading a newspaper that a customer had abandoned in one of the booths. "Been slapping her around again, huh, Spanner?" he inquired when he noticed the bandages on H.J.'s forehead and cheek.

"You're looking especially dapper tonight," returned Ben. "Are you shaving every three days now?"

"I love comedy." Fagin returned to the paper, after flicking ashes on the floor.

When they were seated in a remote booth, H.J. said, "I think I was a little groggy there at Kathkart's. Fill me in, Ben."

"Let's see. Joe Sankowitz got worried when he didn't hear from me by nine." He caught the attention of the blonde waitress and pantomimed an order of two cups of coffee. "Joe took his copies of the photos to—"

"I didn't know he kept any."

"Just two blowups. That's how he identified Zepperman."

"I'm still not clear how Zepperman—"

"Later. Anyway, Joe showed the photos to Ryerson and told him— cleaning up the details considerably—what was going on. Ryerson decided, without alerting the Westport police, to drop by Kathkart's and see why you and I were lingering there."

"But as he arrived, the Westport cops got there, too."

"Apparently even in liberal, funloving Westport you can't shoot off a shotgun without annoying at least some of your neighbors," said Ben. "In fact, I think I have an idea who it was who phoned the police to complain about the noise."

The waitress brought their coffee, whispering to Ben, "I'll try to sneak you free refills if I can."

"Don't risk your life for us, Evie."

H.J. stirred half a spoonful of sugar into her coffee. "Where do I stand in all this?"

"The Westport police want a statement from you sometime tomorrow, but apparently nobody's going to charge you with anything," he told her. "The version of reality that Joe sold Ryerson—and that I expanded on while the paramedic was patching you up—is that Rick Dell gave you the photographs to look after. When people started ransacking your house, you got frightened and came to me. I, of course, advised you to go to the police, but instead you decided to go away for a few days and hide."

"But Chico and the other one trailed me, kidnapped me and brought me to Kathkart's."

"Exactly, and I suspected as much and followed you there. You were never a blackmailer, you and I never practiced graverobbing on Long Island." He took a sip of his coffee. "God, this is awful."

"We could go to my place for coffee—or yours."

Ben looked directly at her. "I wanted to have this talk on neutral ground," he said. "Before we get together again I'd like a few days alone to brood."

"I can understand that," she said, trying the coffee and wincing. "What exactly are you going to be brooding about? Whether or not to ever let me cross your theshold again?"

"Not exactly." He sipped his coffee. "I'm going to have a doughnut. Want one?"

"I suppose I ought to eat something. I don't recall eating since early this morning."

He pantomimed two doughnuts. "During the past few days my life has been somewhat more action packed than usual. Also been more fun, though. That's all due to you, but I'm not yet sure I can handle it all the time."

"I'm not likely to get us involved with murder again soon," she pointed out. "Furthermore, swear to God, I'm not ever going to try blackmail. It's too painful and too risky."

"Have *you* thought about the possibility of our getting together again?" he asked. "I know the other night, when you were trying to con me so you could swipe the pictures, you implied that—"

"I wasn't conning you," she insisted. "Well, not about that anyway. I truly have missed you. Compared to men like Rick Dell, you're a shining—"

"Compared to Rick Dell the Boston Strangler would look like a good deal."

Reaching across the table, smiling, she took his hand. "I haven't made any wise choices in men lately," she admitted. "But I still think that when I agreed to marry you way back when, that was a smart move. So, if you come around to deciding you'd like to try again—marriage, living together or whatever, let me know."

"Okay, that's fine. I will." He paused as the waitress delivered their doughnuts. "What's that atop mine, Evie?"

"Coconut."

"It's green."

"Fagin thought it would be festive if he dyed the coconut."

H.J. took a bite of her doughnut. Chewing, she said,

"While you're brooding, I'll be moping around my studio finishing up my latest lousy romance cover."

"You're going to have to get rid of the notion that your paintings aren't any good."

"Let's not," she suggested, "end the evening with an argument."

$\triangledown$

27

THE PHONE CALL CAME the following Monday. Ben had slept, still alone, until almost ten. The day was grey and a thin misty rain was falling.

He rose out of bed, somewhat reluctantly, and found his way into the bathroom. "Let's see who I am this morning," he said, risking a look in the mirror. "A puffy Ben Spanner. That's not as bad as it might be."

He hadn't talked to H.J. since they'd sat around in Fagin's the night of the kidnapping. He thought about her a lot and he was about ready to come to a decision.

As he felt around on the counter for his electric razor, the phone rang.

He ran back into the bedroom, grabbed up the bedside receiver. "Hello?"

"It's Elsie," announced his agent.

"You shouldn't have tipped me off, that's the very name I was going to guess. What's happening?"

"This is somewhat odd, Ben."

"Odder than the usual job offers I get?"

"Let me know his this strikes you, okay? The Forman & McCay agency is getting ready a major pitch for a new account. You may not want to touch this, but considering all the publicity you and Helen have been getting these past few days it might be terrific for you."

"Whoa now, Elsie. Are you telling me Forman & McCay's going after the My Man Chumley account?"

"Yes, they are. Several agencies are trying for it, after what happened with LM&L. Arthur Moon and Les Beaujack indicted for murder and all," his agent said. "Anyhow, the word I get is that Forman & McCay have the best chance of landing it."

"And they want me for what part?"

She coughed. "My Man Chumley."

He laughed. "As an actor on camera?"

"No, they're going to go with animation. Sounds like a good approach to me, what with all the negative publicity Kathkart and his image have been getting since the whole story broke," she said. "A cute appealing animated version of Chumley could diffuse a lot of the negative feelings."

"So they want me to do the voice of this new, sanitized Chumley?"

"That's right, Ben. This is, when you stop to think about it, a nice touch. The man who exposed the earlier Chumley as a multiple murderer taking over the part."

"How would Walden Foods feel about me? If I'd kept quiet, none of this would have hit the fan."

"Apparently they're a very fundamentalist and upright group. The idea of your taking over as Chumley appeals to them."

"Forman & McCay has already hinted at the idea to the client?"

"So they tell me. Well?"

"If I get the job, it won't be an exclusive thing, will it? I want to be able to keep doing other voice work."

"You can work for any other account that'll have you. You just can't play rival butlers."

"What do they need for the pitch?"

"You'll have to do a demo tape, reading the copy for three proposed animated spots. They'll play those and show storyboards. The fee they're mentioning is extremely handsome."

"I'll never have to do any personal appearances at My Man Chumley restaurants—or actually eat any fish or chips?"

"Nobody will ever see you at all. It's the cartoon Chumley who'll be getting all the attention."

"When do they want to tape them?"

"On Wednesday in Manhattan. At the agency—can you make that?"

"Sure, what time?"

"Eleven. And they want to take you to lunch afterwards, that's Forman and McCay themselves."

"Sounds like I've arrived."

"As far as the agency's concerned, you definitely have. All in all, Benjamin, this seems to me like a fine career move for you."

"That it does."

"I'll phone you later on today if I have any further news. They'll be Fed-Exing you the scripts."

"Righto, love."

He put the phone down. Sitting on the bed, he started to laugh.

After a moment he took up the phone again. "H.J. has got to hear about his," he said and dialed her number.